ULTIMATE GUIDE TO MODERN PARENTING

A gold-medallist, **Pradeep Kapoor** (MBBS, MD) is a paediatrician based in Bhopal. He is an established name in the field of parenting, having written several highly successful books. His first, *Make Your Child a Winner*, is a bestseller and has been translated into seven languages. His novel, *Fosla*, is a humorous take on life in a medical college, and is a rage among readers, both young and old.

A popular medical teacher, **Neelkamal Kapoor** (MBBS, MD) is Dean Research at the All India Institute of Medical Sciences (AIIMS), Bhopal. She is a professor and head of the Department of Pathology and Laboratory Medicine. She is a World Health Organisation (WHO) Fellow and also a Rotary Group Study Exchange (GSE) Fellow. Her book, *Commonsense Parenting*, is a big hit among parents. Besides her eminence in the field of medicine, she also writes stories, features and articles on health and other issues. To her children, she is a very supportive, accepting and fun mother.

ULTIMATE GUIDE TO MODERN PARENTING
RAISING A WINNER WITH EXPERT TIPS...
and a little common sense

Pradeep Kapoor **and** Neelkamal Kapoor

RUPA

Published by
Rupa Publications India Pvt. Ltd 2018
7/16, Ansari Road, Daryaganj
New Delhi 110002

Sales centres:
Allahabad Bengaluru Chennai
Hyderabad Jaipur Kathmandu
Kolkata Mumbai

ISBN: 978-93-5304-768-9

First impression 2018

10 9 8 7 6 5 4 3 2 1

The moral right of the authors has been asserted.

To
Anvika
&
Avanee

CONTENTS

FOUR: ISSUES RELATED TO SCHOOL/SCHOOLING

FIVE: EXPERTS' TIPS TO BRING UP YOUR CHILD BETTER

INTRODUCTION

Children are a versatile combination of Vasco da Gama and Archimedes both rolled into one potent package. They are driven by curiosity and the spirit of adventure. If and when this will turn into a 'misadventure' simply depends upon the parents' bad luck.

Parenting is an art, which relies heavily on the use of common sense. The latter can be loosely defined as the most predictable response to a given situation. A majority of the people in the community would be expected to behave in that manner. However, as someone said in a lighter vein: 'Common sense is not so common'. Looking at the faulty parenting techniques frequently adopted by parents, this observation somehow rings true. All said, there are no set rules which can guarantee a predictable outcome. Each child is unique and requires an individualized approach. What works for Karan may not work for Arjun. Despite this, there are certain guiding principles, which, if followed meticulously, will produce the desired results.

How to make children eat right, get them to do their homework, make them go to bed, wean them off the mobile, teach them discipline, stop them from lying, improve their concentration and memory, boost their self-esteem and augment their communication skills—the challenges for parents are never-ending and they keep changing as the child grows.

Several tricky situations arise on a daily basis in every household, which, if mishandled, can create a major rift between parents and children. The seeds of distrust and anguish sown during one's pre-teens may lead to major maladjustment problems during their adolescence and adulthood. Each of us must know how to deal with children correctly and caringly. All parents want their children to excel and grow into successful adults, but this can be only made possible if they eliminate the weaknesses and reinforce the strengths of their wards.

On the one hand, this book aims at bringing to light, new insights in relation to parenting; on the other, it tries to share positive practices already prevalent in our society. Let us join hands in ensuring that all children get optimal love, care and guidance at home, at school and in the society.

P.S.: All the names mentioned in this book are fictional and have been used only to illustrate a point.

Dr Pradeep Kapoor
Dr Neelkamal Kapoor

ONE

COMMON CONCERNS OF PARENTS

1

MY BABY VS. HER BABY

First-time mother, Ankita Kumar, returned from the hospital with her bundle of joy, feeling blissful. She was ecstatic, and everything seemed nice and beautiful. Then late one night, her little one suddenly decided to wake her up and give her the first test of parenthood. It cried non-stop, didn't want milk and was not wet either. *Well!*

She made her baby lie in her lap and the crying stopped, while two little eyes focused on her face. However, the moment she tried to put it down, it started shrieking again.

When this cycle of waking up, crying and remaining awake for long hours during the night repeated itself on a regular basis, Ankita started getting worried. *Is the little one all right? Can it be colic or gas that is disturbing the sleep? Is my baby developing normally?*

Ankita rushed to her doctor, her mind in turmoil. After a brief examination, and with a broad smile, the doctor declared that her baby was in the pink of health. He also told her, 'Actually, the little fellow does not want to sleep in the night. Your baby's sleep rhythm—the pattern of sleeping in the night and remaining awake during the day—is not yet established.'

Ankita told the doctor that many of her friends' babies had slept well during the night, ever since they were born.

'Why doesn't my child follow the same pattern?'

The answer to this question is that even newborn babies may have differences in their sleep patterns. However, by the age of three months, most babies develop a normal pattern of sleeping in the night and staying awake during daytime.

Feeding is another important and contentious issue for most parents. 'My baby takes ages to finish her bottle of milk, while my friend's child finishes it off in one go,' complained Pariniti to her doctor. 'She also frequently vomits it out.'

Like sleep, feeding patterns also vary from baby to baby. On top of that, some babies are lactase-deficient (lactase is an enzyme necessary for the digestion of milk). They develop stomach cramps and bloating the moment they are fed milk. These babies can only tolerate milk in small quantities, but they should be fed at frequent intervals to fulfil their total daily requirement.

It must be remembered that babies differ not only in their behaviour patterns but also in their reactions to a particular kind of stimuli. Some are startled at even slight sounds or cry if sunlight hits their face, while others are seemingly insensitive to such stimulation. These subtle differences indicate that different personality traits are present in the babies right from the time of birth itself and are a manifestation of their different genetic endowment.

During conception, when the ovum of the female is fertilized by the sperm of the male, the new being receives a genetic inheritance, which influences the development of some traits more than others. Although this influence is most noticeable in physical features, such as the colour of the eyes and hair, the shape of the nose, and the build and complexion, it also appears to play an influential role in reaction tendencies and sensitivity to various situations. These unique reactions to various stimuli are carried forward from infancy to young adulthood.

Thus, it's common sense not to fall into the trap of my baby versus her baby.

ROLE OF ENVIRONMENT IN A CHILD'S GROWTH

The basic personality inherited by the child is also greatly influenced by the environment in which he or she lives. In other words, a child's genetic inheritance interacts with, and is shaped by, the environmental factors operative in the child's world. This interaction results in the emergence of a self-image or personality of the child. Self-image is responsible for directing the further development and behaviour of the child.

A child interacts with various other persons, typically beginning with family members and going on to include the peer group. Other important people who are constantly in close contact with the child (such as grandparents, teachers, etc.) also influence the process of personality development. Much of a child's personality develops on the basis of experiences with these key persons. A child who is rejected and mistreated is likely to develop quite differently from one who is encouraged and loved.

Why are some children reserved and shy, and others, open and loving? Why do some run away from their homes, while others are well adjusted to their home situation? Answers to these and several such questions can be found in the child's environment. The behaviour patterns children learn depend heavily on models to which they are exposed. The socio-cultural environment is the source of differences as well as similarities in personality development. Like a child who is a part of the National Cadet Corps (NCC) or a Scout group will, most likely, develop as a positive person. Qualities such as leadership, discipline and camaraderie are inculcated in the child as a result of his/her participation in such group activities. On the other hand, a child who gets involved with a delinquent gang mostly develops negative traits such as stealing, lying and smoking. It is not difficult to imagine—especially if no corrective measures are taken—what kind of human being that child is going to turn into.

Pranay, who is 7, can pluck the strings of a guitar and can even hum a song or two. It's the influence of his neighbourhood, where a music teacher conducts music classes. Ranjan, 5, is quite adept at cursing and some of his uttering can put even goons to shame. He didn't have to take 'tuition' for learning these invectives; a drunkard father provided him with free tutorials.

It's an undisputed fact of life that we can't escape our socio-cultural milieu. Our genetic endowment provides potentialities for our development, but the shaping of this potential—in terms of perceiving, thinking, feeling and acting—depends heavily on the inputs we receive from our physical and socio-cultural environment.

The environment leaves its imprints even on the faces of rocks; so, can the delicate human brain escape its vagaries?

IS MY BABY GROWING WELL?

Parents—especially mothers—worry a great deal that their baby is not gaining weight properly. The usual complaint is: 'He/she looks so thin and weak'. This is followed by questions about the baby's diet and the request for a good tonic. While dietary advice is generally useful, tonics may not have a significant role in a baby's growth unless a specific deficiency is present, e.g. anaemia, vitamin D deficiency, etc.

If parents know about the normal growth in a baby and the average increase in weight and height during the initial months, they will not get worried unnecessarily. It must be made clear that the figures given below are only a rough estimate and many babies may exceed or lag behind these parameters.

Pointers for parents

- Most newborn babies lose weight during the first few days, but subsequently, they start gaining weight and regain their birth weight within seven days. Around the seventh day, the child's weight is roughly the same as its birth weight.
- During the first year of their life, a baby grows to triple its birth weight, i.e. a newborn weighing 3 kg should weigh 9 kg on completing 1 year. This never happens again in life,

so don't miss out on this unique opportunity.

- During the first year of their life, the average daily weight gain is 30 g in the first quarter, 20 g in the second and 10 g in the third. If your child gains 900 g per month during the first 4 months, you should be happy, but even if the weight gain is only 300 g per month from the ninth to the twelfth month, you should not be worried.
- Between 4 to 12 years, the average weight gain is about 2 kg per year. Most mothers are unduly and unnecessarily worried about the appetite and weight gain of their children during this phase.
- A child measures approximately 50 cm at birth. Height increases by 25 cm in the first year, 12.5 cm during second, 7.5–10 cm in third, and subsequently, varies between 5–7.5 cm per year, till the age of puberty.
- It is possible to predict the ultimate adult height of children with an error of ±4 cm. James Tanner, a British paediatrician, has suggested that anticipated adult height is approximately double of one's height at 2 years or 1.87 times the height at 3 years.

BOYS		AGE	GIRLS	
Weight (kg)	Height (cm)		Weight (kg)	Height (cm)
3.3	50.5	At the time of birth	3.2	49.9
6	61.1	3 months	5.4	60.2
7.8	67.8	6 months	7.2	66.6
9.2	72.3	9 months	8.6	71.1
10.2	76.1	1 year	9.5	75
12.3	85.6	2 years	11.8	84.5

14.6	94.9	3 years	14.1	93.9
16.7	102.9	4 years	16.0	101.6
18.7	109.9	5 years	17.7	108.4
20.7	116.1	6 years	19.5	114.6
22.9	121.7	7 years	21.8	120.6
25.3	127	8 years	24.8	126.4
28.1	132.2	9 years	28.5	132.2
31.4	137.5	10 years	32.5	138.3
32.2	140	11 years	33.7	142
37	147	12 years	38.7	148

TWO

WHAT KIND OF PARENT ARE YOU?

THE MORAL PARENT

A valueless child develops into a clueless adult. Values—as approved and accepted by the society—must be instilled and reinforced repeatedly by the parents. The way to raise a morally-correct child is to be a moral person yourself. If you're honest, empathetic, truthful, decent and caring, it is most likely that that's what your child would be like. If you lie, cheat, or curse, even occasionally, you are sending wrong signals to your child.

When a child is unable to find uniform value patterns, confusion sets in, and the unlimited energies of childhood remain unutilized. A satisfactory value pattern leads to the development of competencies, a positive self-image and a confident personality. Such a child ultimately succeeds, and the entire family—justifiably so—basks in his/her glory.

So, are you a moral parent?

- Before travelling by train, do you 'train' your children to lie to the ticket-checker about being a year or two younger than their actual ages, to avail 50 per cent discount?
- When you go to places with free entry for babies, do you take your schoolgoing child in your arms to make him

seem younger?

- When a motorist overtakes you from the wrong side, do you curse him with the choicest of invectives and use offensive hand gestures?
- Do you jump red lights, park illegally and enter one-way streets from the wrong side, if the traffic police is not watching?
- You have planned a trip to a hill station or there is a wedding in the family, and your child will miss school. Do you make a distant relative 'drop dead' or arrange a false medical certificate for your child?
- You see your child cheating during a quiz. Do you reprimand the child later or overlook the fact, especially if he wins?
- Do you lie to people on the phone? Sitting comfortably in your home, do you tell the person on the other side that you are out of town?

Children have a keen sense of observation and a sharp memory. Initially, they may be confused by the difference in what you teach and what you practise. But soon enough, they will start following what you practise and overlook what you preach.

How you can help your child develop the right value system

1. Praise Good Behaviour

Complimenting your child when she does something admirable is far more effective in promoting positive values than berating her for doing something wrong. Show her how proud you are of her actions—whether it's telling the truth or sharing a toy—by praising her in front of the whole family.

It's also important to encourage her to feel proud of her

good deeds; eventually, her own satisfaction, rather than your praise, will be her motivation for doing positive things.

2. Storytelling

Plenty of children's books and movies are available with eternal themes of being kind to others and persevering in the face of adversity. Make learning interesting and avoid preaching. Tell older children stories from your youth. They will be able to relate to them better and learn that you once faced the same problems they may be experiencing now.

3. Show Generosity

Children have a natural tendency to be self-seeking and are preoccupied with their own needs and demands. However, with a little persuasion, they can be taught how good it can be to share things with others.

Generosity of the parents can be the best example. Here's an incident that occurred long ago: On a road trip to Mount Abu, we stopped at a roadside eatery to have lunch. It was bitingly cold and we were all appropriately dressed. An old man wearing tattered clothes approached us. At first, our children were frightened. But when we offered him hot tea and an old shawl that we happened to carry, the man smiled and blessed us profusely. When our children saw this, they realized that this was a person in need—not someone dangerous or scary.

4. Respect for Others

Once again, being a good role model is a direct way to teach kids this skill. When you show respect to elders, you are imparting an important lesson to your children. Never use derogatory terms when referring to other people and don't shout at, belittle, or criticize people. When your child sees you respecting others, she will automatically learn to be respectful. Teach your child the habit of saying 'please', 'thank you' and 'excuse me' at an early age.

5. *Honesty*

Preschool children tend to tell imaginary tales without meaning to be deceptive. Between the ages of 5 and 7, most kids realize that lying is wrong. However, they may still lie to avoid punishment or because they want to make themselves look better.

Avoid putting your child in a situation where she is tempted to tell a lie. But if you do catch her telling one, try to stay calm. Overreaction can teach her to lie again to avoid your anger. Instead, forgive her, and say you trust her to do the right thing the next time. More importantly, don't lie yourself, because by doing so, you unwittingly devalue the importance of honesty.

THE FAIR PARENT

Pooja Sinha, 14, is the oldest of three children in the Sinha household. She has a younger brother aged 10 and a sister aged 8. She is secure, serene and well adjusted, both at home and in school. She tends to be dominant and bossy towards her siblings, but is very popular amongst her classmates, who admire her talents for leadership and organization.

Pooja's home represents a pleasant and delectable combination of many factors found to produce an expedient environment for positive personality development in a child. Her parents themselves are well adjusted, outgoing and sociable. They enjoy the company of their children and treat them as individuals. They are capable of appraising their children objectively and in a detached manner; at the same time, they exude warmth, emotionality and devotion towards them, without any hesitation or awkwardness. Every child gets due importance and is treated as an equal member of the family.

Mrs Suman Sinha is a computer professional who operates from her home and does regular piecework for various firms. She is stable, kindly, good-humoured and possesses remarkable patience. Her keen sense of humour enlivens even the dullest of moments, making her family a cheerful lot.

Mr Amit Sinha is a Senior Executive who, in spite of

his busy schedule, never fails to involve himself in the day-to-day running of the household. Dinner time is discussion time, where each member of the 'family council' is present and participates actively in the dialogue. After dinner, coffee for the parents and milk for children is a tradition strictly adhered to. These hot beverages are drunk in the living room, where discussions may hot up, or turn to non-stop laughter and jokes with plenty of leg-pulling, but without the intention of toppling anyone.

It should be emphasized that the Sinha household is not without its routine problems. Mrs Sinha faces the usual disciplinary crises, sibling rivalries, food prejudices and preferences, and general snags faced by most mothers. Because of her more-than-average tolerance and patience, she manages these situations with admirable restraint and calm. Mr Sinha's contribution and involvement helps to lighten her load and brighten her mood.

The Sinha household is quite close to being called an ideal home. Most of the things accomplished by Mr and Mrs Sinha are through the use of common sense, mutual understanding and cooperation. As is apparent, a vibrant and harmonious home is a reflection of the personalities of its members.

According to George Santayana, a Spanish-American novelist, 'The family is one of nature's masterpieces'. The bright dreams of its members and the dark realities of life compete with each other to colour this masterpiece. Family is a microcosm embracing intricate interpersonal relationships. The maintenance of a dynamic equilibrium between the ambitions, demands and commands of the parents and the capabilities, attempts and performances of the children, is obligatory for the sustenance of this little world.

Pointers for parents:

- Be outgoing and sociable.
- Maintain mutual harmony.
- Treat your children as individuals.
- Enjoy their company to the fullest.
- Give due importance to each child.
- Be objective, but exude warmth and love.
- Maintain equilibrium through dialogue and discussion.
- Patience, patience, patience—they are the three attributes of good parenting.

THE UNFAIR PARENT

Deepti Gulati, 10, is a shy, withdrawn and anxious child. She is the youngest of the three sisters and resents her more accomplished elder siblings. She is apprehensive of her mother, and unfortunately, her father has always been a stranger to the household.

By the time Deepti arrived on the scene, Mrs Gulati had already lost whatever little patience she had had with her two elder daughters. Deepti, thus, faced rejection at a very early and vulnerable age. She was left at the mercy of a housemaid when she was hardly 3 months old. Throughout infancy and early childhood, Deepti was looked after by a never-ending procession of maids. Even on her first day at school, her bag and lunch box were arranged haphazardly by an illiterate maid.

At school, Deepti is well behaved to the point of being docile. Her grades are poor and she barely manages to scrape through. Her teachers find her dull, inactive and difficult to communicate with. Her standard response to most commands is, 'I don't know'. Deepti doesn't have many friends; her only real friend is her doll—the two being inseparable. She goes to bed holding the doll in her arms and talks to her late into the night.

Mrs Gulati, Deepti's mother, is an aggressive, domineering woman with a harsh tone. She is given to expressing her opinion fervently and believes in having the last word in any argument. She is self-centred to the point of being selfish. She indulges herself with a lot of sleep and enjoys her kitty parties and card sessions. Shopping and going to the movies with her friends are her favourite pastimes. With extreme dexterity, she has modified her entire home, her children and her businessman-husband, to suit her life of leisure and irresponsible abundance.

Actually, Mrs Gulati is irritated by children and doesn't have much patience with her three daughters. For her, the model child is the quiet, unobtrusive one—to be seen around the house, but not heard. She imposes strict discipline and rigid standards of behaviour. Her arbitrary commands always keep the children on tenterhooks and her sarcasm lashes out at them from every corner of the house.

Deepti remains Mrs Gulati's favourite victim. If she eats an ice cream, her mother says, 'I am sure you're going to spill it all over your frock'. If she opens the fridge to take a bottle of water, her mother says, 'I suppose you are going to drop the bottle on the floor'. If she sits down to do homework, Mrs Gulati says, 'I know you will make mistakes in every line'. Thus, Mrs Gulati shatters little Deepti's confidence with her harsh words and makes her feel worthless.

Depending on her mood, Mrs Gulati sometimes indulges in jokes and horseplay with the children, but when her good mood passes, she flares up with sudden anger and clamps down heavily on the girls. Swooping down like an eagle, she generally manages to catch hold of the youngest bird and mauls her. This irrational and unpredictable outburst totally confuses the children as to what is permitted and what is forbidden.

When Deepti won a prize in the painting competition at

school, it was pooh-poohed by Mrs Gulati. In her rush to attend a party, she pushed away her daughter and her little trophy.

Most children subjected to maternal deprivation are not those separated from their mothers, but rather the ones who suffer from inadequate or distorted maternal care. Here, the mother typically neglects, devotes little attention to, and is generally callous with, the child.

Such rejection may manifest itself in several ways in the parents' (or in this case, the mother's) behaviour(s) towards the child: Through physical neglect, denial of love and affection, lack of interest in the child's activities and achievements, harsh or inconsistent disciplinary measures, failure to spend time with the child, lack of respect for the child's feelings and sometimes, cruel and abusive treatment.

In Deepti's case, the rejection is:

- Complete (in majority of cases it is partial)
- Active (it is generally passive)
- Overtly cruel (subtle cruelty is more common)

Children of cold and rejecting mothers suffer from:

- Feeding problems
- Persistent bedwetting
- Excessive aggression/fears
- Poor and slow conscience development
- Diminished intelligence during early school years
- The tendency to lie and steal
- Delinquent habits and the tendency of running away from home

An unpleasant emotional environment and lack of encouragement at home has a grossly inhibiting and suppressing effect on a child's intellectual development and functioning. It is seen that many adults who were rejected in childhood have serious difficulty in giving and receiving affection.

Why do parents reject their children?

It seems that a large proportion of such parents have themselves been the victims of parental rejection. In this sense, lack of love can be called a 'congenital disease'. Various studies show that parental rejection leads to feelings of insecurity and inadequacy, retarded conscience and general intellectual development, low self-esteem, feelings of loneliness and the inability to give and receive love.

THE OVERINDULGENT PARENT

Dhruv Verma, 13, is an inconsiderate, whimsical little tyrant. He is self-centred, dominating, demanding and thoroughly spoilt. His parents treat him like a king and fulfil all his reasonable/unreasonable demands. His two elder sisters have clear instructions not to annoy him in any way.

Dhruv's father is 'living again' through his son, seeing him as a young replica of himself. He derives extreme satisfaction in gratifying his son's whims and fancies. Dhruv is granted whatever he wants, no matter what sacrifices are made by other members of the family.

Dhruv is the 'apple of the eye' of Mrs Verma. She dotes on him, and treats him with lavish kisses and luscious dishes. She is not bothered that, at 13, her son already weighs over 60 kg.

Dhruv, for his part, has learned to exploit his parents by skilfully and craftily using tactics such as crying, loving, being cute or being well behaved, and when all else fails, simply by throwing a tantrum. In fact, he is the one in command at home and manages his sisters and parents quite easily by his deft manipulations.

When Dhruv's privileged and pampered status at home did not transfer automatically to the outside world, it came as a shock to him. Teased by his peers and nicknamed 'Fatso', initially he was confused but later developed extreme agitation and aggressive tendencies. He often fought with schoolmates and rebelled against his teachers' disciplinary measures. His parents were reprimanded by the school authorities but things did not improve. Gradually, Dhruv become an anxious, unhappy and maladjusted child at school, while at home, he remained a selfish and impatient 'super-brat'.

Overindulgent parents not only spoil their children but also spoil their chances of successfully adjusting in life. Over-permissiveness and lack of discipline at home has been correlated positively with antisocial and aggressive behaviours, particularly during middle and later childhood. In dealing with authority, such children are usually rebellious since they have been used to having their own way and this often lands them in trouble. Such children approach problems in an aggressive and demanding manner and get frustrated easily.

Prudence in indulgence, through the use of common sense, would have prevented Dhruv's predicament. Parents must maintain equilibrium while bringing up children. This is absolutely necessary if their children are to develop a balanced and practical approach to life.

THE OVERPROTECTIVE PARENT

Anurag Mishra, 12, is a fearful, dependent and submissive child. Right from birth, his mother took control of his life and gave him little autonomy or freedom. Throughout infancy and childhood, Anurag was kept in a 'germ-free environment'. All other children were not 'good enough' to play with him— they were dirty, infectious, bad-mannered or 'contaminating' in some way or the other. The concept of 'hygiene' and the fear of bacteria are so deeply engrained in his mind that while going to school, on a picnic or to the movies, he might forget his spectacles but he never fails to carry a bottle of hand sanitizer with him.

Anurag's mother doesn't want him to risk injury or face defeat by playing with 'evil' boys living in the neighbourhood. So he plays cricket with his father in their backyard. As it is, he is not allowed to remain outdoors for too long, because of his supposedly frail health. He is always over-clothed, and medicines are poured down his throat with alarming regularity.

Till the age of 4, Anurag was always carried in the arms of his parents. At 5, he was still being breast-fed at night. His mother would insist upon bathing him and putting on his clothes even till the age of 10.

Maternal overprotection, or 'Momism'—especially if the

father is approving of, or complacent to, this 'smothering' of the child—makes the child totally dependent. Such a child lacks initiative, seeks help whenever faced with any problem, avoids competition and doesn't derive satisfaction from work.

The 4-year-old who does not feed him/herself, the 5-year-old who doesn't play with peers unattended by the mother or the 6-year-old who doesn't dress him/herself are all exhibiting dependence. The overprotective attitude of parents of such children needs urgent modification if the children are to develop independence and self-confidence.

In shielding the child from every danger, parents deny him the opportunities to learn by testing the realities. Overprotection indirectly implies that they regard the child as incapable of coping with everyday problems. Such children grow up into insecure individuals, who feel threatened by the world. They have feelings of inadequacy, their intellectual striving is severely compromised and they generally suffer from a low self-esteem.

While it's expected of parents to warn the children of dangerous situations and undesirable friends, it is foolish on their part to take all of the child's decisions. This deprives them of the opportunity to learn through experimentation—the only sure-shot method of gaining permanent knowledge. Common sense advises to let children take their own decisions, especially in cases where it will not be associated with dangerous consequences, even if the child goes wrong.

THE OVER-DEMANDING PARENT

Gaurav Nigam is not even 15 and already considers himself a failure. 'Gaurav' means 'glory'; this is what he was supposed to bring to the family. His parents are determined, pushy professionals who expect him to top in the class, excel in sports and win prizes in debates and dramatics. The Nigam household either has an air of 'great expectations' or gloom of 'spectacular disappointments' linked to Gaurav's performance.

Initially, Gaurav tried to live up to his parents' unrealistically-high expectations. But no matter how hard he tried, he seemed to fail in the eyes of his parents. When he improved his rank from tenth to third, he was asked, 'Why didn't you rank first in the class?' Ultimately, he couldn't cope with the sustained pressure and gave up. The unrealistic demands of his parents became the albatross around his neck. The pain and frustration of not being good enough led to self-devaluation and Gaurav eventually came to feel: 'I can't do it, so why try?'

Characteristics of over-demanding parents:
- They have very high expectations.
- For them it's ALL work and NO play.
- They have an extreme commitment to success.

- They believe in rules, rules and more rules.
- They are generally disconnected from the needs of their children.

By their excessive demands, these parents promote failure and also tend to discourage further effort on the part of the child. Where the child has the capacity for exceptionally high-level performance, despite the demands, things may work out; but even here, the child may be pushed so much that little room is left for spontaneity or development as an independent person. In some instances, parents who are not successful, focus on the child to meet their own need for success.

Life isn't like the touchscreen of a smartphone where everything is condensed into megapixels. It is a huge canvas which provides ample opportunities to paint one's masterpiece. Common sense dictates that Gaurav's perceived failures should have been overlooked by his parents. By not doing so, they not only failed to encourage their child, but inadvertently harmed his self-esteem and future prospects.

THE PUNITIVE PARENT

Mohit Singh, 13, has changed three schools in the last two years, due to his poor performance. He was admitted to the present one in the hope that the promised 'personalized attention' would help him overcome his problems. Here again, he is lagging behind in the class without any signs of improvement.

During the last parent-teacher meeting, Mr Singh, his policeman-father, showed his displeasure and disappointment at Mohit's grades. He complained that his hopes were belied, and the tall promises made at the time of admission and taking of donation, were not fulfilled.

Pragati Tandon, a Child Counsellor attached to the school, was asked to talk to Mr and Mrs Singh and take Mohit under her direct charge. She submitted the following report to the Principal:

> Mr Singh, Deputy Superintendent Police, is a somewhat arrogant, irritable and easily excitable person who finishes all arguments with an emphatic wave of his hands. Mrs Singh is a timid, homely woman, who believes in walking one step behind her husband. Mr Singh returns home from his duty at odd, unearthly hours and the

slightest noise or disturbance at home makes him explode into a violent rage. He is a harsh disciplinarian who has a 'hands on' approach to all problems of children. He beats Mohit mercilessly on any pretext and even the slightest misdemeanour on Mohit's part has never been spared. During my conversation with him, Mr Singh declared with odd pride that: 'I don't have to hit Mohit any more; my loud voice is enough to make him wet his pants.' Mohit is terrified of his father and suffers from anxiety, insecurity and feelings of worthlessness. He hates his father, and several times, has fantasized about killing him with a knife. He has also contemplated running away from home. Mohit lacks initiative, spontaneity and is not a friendly child. He lacks warmth in his dealings and tends to be aggressive. To get even with his father, he deliberately underperforms in the examinations. He feels that this is one way by which he can get back at his father.

Six months and several counselling sessions later, Mr Singh was made to realize that his excessively harsh discipline and beatings were the reason behind Mohit's poor performance. It was his behaviour that required changing and not his child's school. Thankfully, Mr Singh changed his conduct and today Mohit is a happy child who is performing very well in his studies.

It has been well documented that punishment is associated with greater child dependency, more aggressiveness and a slower development of conscience. Extreme parental punitiveness appears to make the child emotionally unstable, hateful and less sociable. The unhappy effects of punishment run like a dismal streak throughout the later life of a child.

It is not uncommon to come across over-strict fathers and submissive mothers like Mr and Mrs Singh. The harsh discipline, combined with insufficient moral and emotional support, can play havoc with the personality of a child in such homes. Fortunately, with increasing financial independence, mothers are now in a better position to put things in the right perspective.

THE HELICOPTER PARENT

Helicopter parents are so named because, like helicopters, they hover overhead, keeping a close watch on their child's life. These parents try their best to always keep track of their child's activities, experiences and problems, especially at educational institutions. Such parents frequently contact the teachers to complain about the grades of their child. Helicopter parents continue to interfere in their child's career even at college level and are not averse to trying to influence them in their professional life and during salary negotiations. Helicopter parents attempt to ensure that their children are on a path to success by paving it for them. They are obsessed with preventing failure at all costs. The term was coined by child psychologist, Dr Haim Ginott. In his book, *Between Parent and Teenager,* a teen complains: 'Mother hovers over me like a helicopter.'

Most parents let go of minor issues, but helicopter parents just won't buzz off. These parents are sometimes helpful, sometimes annoying and always hovering over their children and making noise. They are incredibly close to their children, which may not be such a bad thing, but inadvertently, they subvert the independent thinking and growth of their child. Such children fail to fend for themselves even though they may be capable of doing so.

The rise of helicopter parenting has coincided with the current boom in the economy, with low unemployment and higher disposable income. The advocacy by a section of parenting experts, for increased child engagement probably also has a role to play in the rise of this phenomenon. Fewer children (one or two per family) might also have been an aggravating factor.

These parents are physically 'hyper-present' but psychologically absent. Helicopter parenting results in too much presence, and it is the wrong kind of presence. Children may interpret it as interference in their daily affairs and may revolt. The parents do it with good intentions, but generally with bad results, because without realizing, they become rigid and authoritarian in their approach.

The advent of mobile phones may be a contributing factor in the rise of helicopter parenting. It will not be wrong to call the mobile phone the world's longest umbilical cord. Studies have shown that overprotective, overbearing or over-controlling parents can cause long-term mental health problems for their children. The effects of these mental health problems may possibly be lifelong, make the child feel insecure and leave her less able to regulate her own behaviour.

Common sense says that parents should avoid hovering constantly over their children. Helicopters are meant to hover in the skies, not over children.

THREE
....
COMMON CHILDHOOD ISSUES

DEMYSTIFYING INFERIORITY COMPLEX

Inferiority complex is a complex subject. In this chapter we have tried to demystify its complexities. Parents should be aware of this situation and must take immediate measures to prevent this problem from taking root in their child. Overcoming inferiority complex is difficult and it generally leaves behind some ill effects. So, common sense tells us to focus on preventing its development.

Inferiority complex or low self-esteem is variously defined as poor self-image, feeling of worthlessness, sense of insecurity, state of self-doubt, timidity and so on. It is a major hurdle in the path to success and glory, and can become a stumbling block for many a potential winner.

High self-esteem is feeling good about oneself, knowing one's strengths and weaknesses, accepting them and acting in accordance with them. However, it should not be confused with an inflated ego, which is the prime reason behind the premature ending of many promising careers.

Success and self-esteem have a close and direct relationship. Success is important for the growth of positive feelings about the self and affirmation of worth. A child with high self-esteem can use a failure as a learning experience while a child with low self-esteem gets bogged down. Everyone experiences 'lows' and 'highs'. On some days we feel more confident, while on others, we are down in the dumps. Feeling less sure and suffering from doubts from time to time is all right, but persistent feelings of worthlessness and insecurity are a matter of grave concern.

Children with high/low self-esteem

1. ***Children with High Self-esteem***: These children are able to express their feelings and emotions in a controlled, ascendant manner. They generally succeed in influencing other people's behaviours in a positive way. These children approach new challenges with confidence and show a lot of independence and responsibility. They don't get easily frustrated by failures, and view them in proper perspective. Through persistence and perseverance they turn failures into resounding success. Children with high self-esteem are full of ideas and inspiration and are able to control their environment through their positive approach.

2. ***Children with Low Self-esteem***: These children are low on confidence and generally speak in self-derogatory terms. They go on the defensive easily and avoid situations which may cause confrontation and tension. They are unable to form opinions and rely on others' judgments. To counter doubts about themselves, they constantly blame others for their problems and failures. They are not open to reason and feel powerless when faced with any challenging situation. They avoid new experiences and shy away from interactions. Children with low self-esteem have low frustration tolerance; thus they tend to give up without putting in a worthwhile effort. These children usually use the crutches of fate and luck to plod along an ill-defined path that leads nowhere.

The 'how' and 'why' of inferiority complex

Every child has the potential to excel, but whether they will succeed in later life depends upon a complex interplay of several inter-related factors. Children develop positive personalities only if they are encouraged by people and circumstances which ensure that their self-esteem is carefully nourished throughout the crucial growing-up years. Genetic endowment, or the potential to succeed, may be present but it can be blocked by adverse environmental factors operating at home, at school and in society. When this happens, it results in a collapse of confidence and withdrawal from the struggle towards worthwhile achievement.

One adverse factor may have little or no effect, especially if it is brief and occurs in the context of an otherwise healthy and nurturing family environment. The development of inferiority complex and consequent failures become increasingly likely if there are more factors operating and they continue over a longer period of time.

Predisposing factors

1. *Faulty Parental Attitudes*

   - Lack of communication
   - Rejection
   - Harsh discipline
   - Unrealistic demands
   - Undue comparison
   - Overprotection

2. *Dysfunctional Family Situation*

   - Parental discord

- Separation/Divorce
- Death in the family
- Frequently moving family
- Parental loss of job
- Parental addiction

3. *Maladjustment at School*

- Peer pressure
- Peer rejection
- Punitive teachers
- Style of teacher versus style of student
- Language difficulties
- Slow learner

4. *Others*

- Sibling performance
- Health-related problems, e.g. asthma, obesity, etc.
- Abuse
- Learning disabilities
- Traumatic emotional development
- Odd surname, dark complexion, use of spectacles, etc.

Timid, anxious children lacking in confidence, despite their superior intelligence, generally underachieve. They are unable to realize their potential and regard themselves as failures. This further undermines their confidence and damages their self-esteem. Thus, a vicious circle is formed which is difficult to break.

Probably the most common comment made by teachers in the report cards of children is: 'Could do better'. Much is made of the child's inability to cope with examinations by many teachers and parents. Constant reminders to the child at school and home, that he is careless and does not work hard enough, can only make him lose heart and create doubts in his mind about himself.

Some parents put excessive pressure on their children by subjecting them to unrealistic demands. If children fail to measure up to parental expectations, they lose faith in their own abilities. Repeated failures erode self-confidence, and gradually the child develops a maladjusted personality burdened with low self-esteem.

Undue comparison is a potent weapon in the hands of parents, by which they can cause serious and permanent damage to the child's self-esteem. Parents keep citing the example of children who are brilliant in studies and outstanding in sports. They do this in the hope of motivating their children to perform better, but it generally has the opposite effect. Mostly the child's performance worsens. There can be two reasons for this. Firstly, the child underperforms deliberately to show his revolt against parental dictates. The child resents praise for peers, especially when it comes from his parents. Secondly, the child may be genuinely incapable of performing up to the parents' high expectations. Thus, unnecessary and unjustified comparisons can only harm the child's self-image.

Faulty discipline and low self-esteem have a symbiotic relationship—both thrive together. Whether it is excessively harsh, inconsistent or over-permissive, flawed discipline will harm the child's personality. It has been observed that in the long run, punishment is ineffectual as a technique for eliminating the kind of behaviour against which it is directed. Punishment tends to orient the child away from reality, and makes him insecure and more dependent on adult affection and attention. Effective use of discipline is the key to successful adjustments in life.

Many children develop profound worries relating to persistent parental discord. They fear that this will lead to divorce and abandonment. Generally, these anxieties are not based on reality but may be due to comparisons with classmates from so-called 'broken homes' or a direct consequence of the innumerable 'family-soaps' shown on the idiot box. Parental illness/unemployment and financial hardship can also prevent an all-round personality development of the child.

Anxiety, due to any cause, can adversely affect self-image. Anxious children are self-depreciating, low on confidence and unable to face day-to-day challenges. They also tend to be low on curiosity and adventurousness and while away their time daydreaming. These children are taunted by peers and scorned by teachers. With such an all-encompassing negative environment, it is not difficult to understand why these children get trapped in the vicious cycle of inferiority complex.

Parental messages and utterings are deeply ingrained in children's minds and have a potent effect on their future scholastic achievements and social adjustments. If children are repeatedly told that they are no good, they presume it to be a true evaluation of their worth. Gradually, the feeling of inferiority takes root and these children start believing that they are worthless.

Common sense tells us to talk *to* our children, not talk *down to* them.

13

SEVEN STEPS TO BUILD YOUR CHILD'S SELF-ESTEEM

One of the most precious gifts you can give your children—from infants to adolescents—is a sense of self-worth. By improving your child's self-esteem you offer him a more positive future. For accomplishing this, you must first evaluate your own feelings of self-esteem. If you yourself suffer from feelings of inadequacy, you will find it extremely difficult to help your child. You must believe in yourself, have faith in your child's capabilities and view things positively.

The following recommendations to improve your child's self-esteem should be applied with consistency and discretion. It must be remembered that no single suggestion by itself can make a significant impact. Moreover, several other factors, which may not be within your control, such as peer pressure, teachers' attitudes, etc., will also affect the child's self-esteem. However, your genuine desire to help your child will ultimately decide his fate.

1. Find solutions, not faults

Are you quick to point a finger at your child if he makes a mistake? Do you constantly criticize the child for his behaviour? If yes, then you are sending wrong messages to your child. Parents who merely blame the child for his faults and fail to teach correct behaviour, cause irreparable damage to their child's self-esteem. These children never learn to handle difficult situations and get easily frustrated and disheartened.

Instead of highlighting faults, parents should be fixing them. They should try to ensure that the mistakes and misbehaviour do not recur, and give the child the opportunity to realize and analyse his mistakes. This makes children more responsible and resilient and they gradually learn the right behaviour and develop the right attitude.

2. Use rewards, avoid punishment

Rewards reinforce desired behaviour, while punishments strengthen feelings of worthlessness. All children want to win parental approval. Some make it quite obvious by their continuous striving; others project an indifferent exterior, but may work towards gaining parental praise in their own secretive way. The onus of recognizing, appreciating and rewarding children's efforts lies on the parents.

Throughout this book, we have repeatedly advocated the use of a reward system in the hope that parents will adopt it and use it more often. Rewards need not always be monetary or in the form of gifts. Praise, show of affection or a pat on the back works equally well and is quite effective in generating feelings of self-worth.

3. Let children take decisions

The ability to think clearly and decide quickly is the hallmark of all successful people. Allowing children to take decisions that affect their daily life gives them an opportunity to exercise control and enhance their self-esteem. It also makes them more adept at taking major decisions in later life. Decisions about which clothes to wear, toothpaste or soap to use, photographs to use to decorate their own room, friends to invite to the birthday party, menu to be selected—all can help the child grow in confidence. Mistakes are bound to happen but they must be viewed positively and utilized as learning experiences.

4. Don't handle kids with 'kid gloves'

Each time you rush to the aid of your child, you underline his incompetence and undermine his confidence. In doing so, you are inadvertently reinforcing feelings of low self-esteem. Some parents have the tendency to 'bail out' their children each time they are confronted with a difficult situation. To prevent children from facing frustration and possible failure, parents try to alter the environment, in an attempt to make it more favourable. In shielding children from every danger, such parents deny them the needed opportunities for reality-testing. These children get a distorted view of the world and may become so dependent that they are unable to meet any challenge without adult help.

The ability to master the environment and find solutions to problems is crucial to the development of a positive self-image. According to acclaimed American dancer Angela Isadora Duncan, 'The finest inheritance you can give a child is to allow it to make its own way, completely on its own feet.' Parents must allow children to explore and experiment. When children are permitted to profit from their own mistakes with minimum adult interference, they tend to be more confident, less dependent on adults and better able to face reality. These children have high self-esteem and strong feelings of self-worth.

5. Leave scope for disagreement

We live in a democratic society, which bestows on us the freedom of speech. As adults we have the independence to agree or disagree with any viewpoint. Should our children be denied this basic right?

Children must be given opportunities to express themselves and register their protests. Parents and teachers should be prepared to listen to a child's point of view. Even when their point of view does not evoke a favourable response, the knowledge that they were given a sympathetic and sincere audience, makes children feel important and worthy. Such opportunities convince children that they have a say in matters concerning them. They come to realize that they have the power to change their environment and mould their destiny.

6. Allow 'success' to succeed

Once a child successfully accomplishes a task, provide him more opportunities to do it again. Let the child repeat successful experiences as it helps build self-esteem. With repeated opportunity and success, a child masters the required skills and develops confidence. Simple tasks such as making tea, boiling eggs, taking telephone messages, fixing something in the house or making the shopping list can be used to repeat success. A proven track record of success is the ultimate proof of high self-esteem.

7. Set realistic goals

Setting realistic goals and helping children achieve them is an important factor in improving self-esteem. Left to themselves, children may set unrealistic goals, fail to achieve them and lose confidence. Once this happens, they become unwilling to venture out and face new challenges. Such children become limited in their experience and are vulnerable to failure. Repeated failures lead to the development of avoidance behaviour and feelings of inferiority.

You must help your children in deciding their priorities and defining their goals. Once you know what the child wants to achieve, prepare a time-bound programme to go about it. Define clearly the steps necessary to reach the goal and treat each step as a smaller goal. If the child gets stuck at any stage, offer him alternative ways to accomplish the task. This will help your child attain his goals with a boosting of self-esteem at every step.

Seven behaviours to avoid

Common sense says that parents who want to improve their child's self-esteem must omit the following seven behaviour patterns:

- Criticism
- Hostility
- Ridicule
- Rejection
- Disapproval
- Discouragement
- Unfairness

14

HOW TO HANDLE CHILDHOOD FEARS

All children have fears. Parents should not get distressed or overly worried by their child's fears, otherwise, inadvertently, they will heighten those dreads and worsen the situation. Certain fears are 'age-appropriate', and only when the child fails to overcome them in due course of time, active intervention should be contemplated.

Some parents refuse to acknowledge and accept a child's fears as a natural part of growing up. They feel that there is something wrong with a fearful child. Their refusal to accept the child's fears makes them appear unkind, but the truth is, somewhere deep down, they have a perception of failing as parents.

A fear of darkness can be found predominantly between 2–3 years of age but may extend well beyond childhood. Many adults also fear stepping out at night because darkness is associated with thefts, murders and other dangerous things. As children enter teenage, the concept of death becomes clear to them. They experience the greatest anxiety about the death of a parent. Several children also develop a fear of going blind or contracting some fatal illness.

It is quite common for children to experience nightmares between the ages of 3–6. The exact reason is not known, but it is believed that they are related to the normal anxiety and stress that are a part of the lives of growing children. After a nightmare, the child needs his/her parents' comfort and support. Get to the child as quickly as possible and once there, stay with the child till he overcomes the nightmare and falls back to sleep. Keep comforting the child by gently stroking his head for some time. Many children remember their dreams the next day. Encourage them to talk about their dreams in the morning. Discuss and suggest ways to overcome the things that frightened them in their dream.

Children these days are also exposed to several anxiety-causing experiences—television violence being one of the major culprits. Ansh, 9, was a well-adjusted, bright and happy child. He was perfectly comfortable sleeping in his room. One evening while his parents were away, he saw a TV programme on a serial child killer. He couldn't sleep that night because of fear and kept a vigil for the murderer. When the light of his parents' room was switched off, he quietly slipped inside it and slept on the floor.

Ansh was so upset by the horror scenes shown on the programme that he lost the courage to sleep alone in his bedroom. Night after night, he started creeping into his parents' room. His parents were also greatly disturbed by this new development.

'Barrier Parenting' may sound like a new and fancy coinage but is essentially an old, time-trusted practice. Parents must actively monitor whether the things going into the child's mind are healthy or unhealthy. Ansh's parents need to discuss the problem with him and reassure him. They should allow him to sleep with them for some time. They must also plan happy experiences to fill his mind. Gradually, over the next few days, they can make him sleep in his room, keeping the night lamp on and any interconnecting door open.

Ways to help children overcome their fears

1. Show Them the Way

Children model their behaviour by observing their parents. Parents who deal confidently with situations which children find intimidating, set a positive example.

During the orthodontic check-up of my 13-year-old daughter, the dentist advised the removal of four teeth to achieve proper alignment. Naturally, she was terrified! Even I am petrified by the sight of some dental instruments. I had been postponing the removal of an impacted tooth for years. But I decided to set an example and steeled myself for the stainless steel dental pliers.

A few days later, my daughter accompanied me to the dentist's clinic and observed my dental extraction pass off smoothly. My calm, composed (and calculated) response helped her gain confidence and gather courage. She completed her orthodontic treatment without much fuss. Actually, the courage she showed during all those extractions was quite remarkable.

It is not necessary that you show courage at all times; rather, sometimes it helps to admit your fear. When you tell your children that you, too, used to be afraid of the dark, they will realize they aren't alone in feeling scared. By seeing that you no longer fear darkness, they will learn an important lesson—fears can be mastered.

2. Never Terrorize a Child

We carry the fears and misgivings of childhood into our adult life. Frightening a child with a lizard or a bearded man can instil a permanent fear in his mind. Such a child withdraws from his environment, becomes a recluse and lacks confidence. He may lose heart easily and give in without putting up a fight. Such a child can also develop a variety of complexes.

It has been observed that up to the age of 3 years, the emotion of fear is not deep-rooted and can be easily removed by the active involvement of parents. But from around 5 years, fear leaves a strong impact on the child's mind and teasing out its effect becomes much more difficult.

When you terrorize your child by saying: 'If you don't study, the lion will eat you', you create a dread in the child's mind. Later, if you take the child to a zoo or a circus, he will be terror-struck at the sight of a lion. Thus, what should have been a happy outing becomes an embarrassment for you and a nightmare for your child.

Parents sometimes use the following kinds of statement to instil fear as a convenient tool to control their children:

- If you don't eat food, the bogeyman will take you away. (Instead, tell him if he doesn't eat food, he will become weak and will not be able to play cricket/football.)
- If you don't stop crying, we will give you to the policeman. (Instead, tell him if he doesn't stop crying, you will not take him to the gaming zone.)
- If you don't drink milk, we will ask the doctor to fill it in his syringe and inject it in your tummy. (Instead, tell him if he doesn't drink milk, his bones will become weak.)

3. Don't Punish or Ridicule a Child For Being Afraid

There is no point in shouting at or punishing a terrified child. This will only increase his fears. Ridiculing a child by calling him names such as coward, cry baby, chicken-hearted or lily-livered, is counterproductive. Look at a child's fear from his point of view, not an adult one.

A ghost may appear quite real to a child. Making fun or saying that such things don't exist will not help in anyway. Instead tell him: 'Lots of children your age are afraid of ghosts. It's alright to feel that way.' At the same time, try to find out what has caused the child to believe in ghosts and plan practical solutions. All children feel more secure when a rational explanation is offered for their fears, even when they do not fully understand it.

4. The Balancing Act

Ignore a child's fears at your own peril; be too solicitous and share your bed. Some children feign being afraid in order to manipulate their parents into letting them sleep in the same bed, to extract more attention or to avoid going to school. Parents have to strike a balance between being too concerned and not bothering at all. Both over-concern and neglect can reinforce a child's fears. If children are rewarded for not being afraid, they will soon overcome their fears—pretended or real.

5. Teasing Out Terror

Children must feel safe at all times. If they appear distressed, talk to them about their fears. Talking about fears gives children the opportunity to work out their fears without shame. Reassure them that fear will diminish and eventually disappear. Stress, due to any cause, can precipitate or accentuate fears. Shifting of family, change of school, death in the family—all can make the child extremely anxious. If parents are understanding and supportive they can reduce the child's anxiety about new circumstances and minimize his fears.

Case Studies

1. Manisha, 13, was mortally afraid of cockroaches. The mere sight of these brown creatures was enough to send her into a frenzy. When she was a young child she was repeatedly threatened that if she didn't drink milk, eat food or complete her homework, cockroaches would climb on her bed and bite her. Slowly, the cockroaches, instead of living in crevices, started living inside her mind.

   To remove her fear, she was shown that just two puffs of an insecticide were enough to kill the cockroaches. She saw for herself that when a cockroach was touched by a stick, it quickly ran away. It took some time, but ultimately, Manisha was able to understand that cockroaches were, after all, tiny little things like all other insects and a big, strong girl like her had no reason to be afraid of them.

2. Rohan, 7, was afraid of dogs and started crying the moment he saw a dog nearby. He was once bitten by a stray dog and had to take anti-rabies injections. His elder brother, Sohan, revelled in terrorizing Rohan with horrifying tales of dangerous dogs.

   To remove the fear of dogs (or any other animal) it is necessary that an environment be built that shows the dog to be a friendly and faithful animal. Here is how Rohan's parents helped him overcome his fear of dogs:

   - Sohan was reprimanded and forbidden from frightening Rohan.
   - A framed poster was put up in the children's room, showing a young child reclining comfortably against

a dog and sipping water from his bottle.
- Rohan was given a toy dog to play with.
- A storybook about a friendly, faithful and brave dog was presented and read to him.
- Rohan was taken to the nearby park quite often to let him see other children playing with their pets.

3. Sushmita, 9, was scared of the dark. Moreover, the shadows a nearby tree cast in her bedroom, the fluttering of curtains in the gentle breeze, all combined to create a horrifying illusion. She would remain awake and keep her bedroom lights on, or plead with her parents to let her sleep in their bedroom.

   Her parents couldn't accept her fear: 'There is nothing to be afraid of; go back to sleep', was their usual, irritated response. They should have realized that the shadows were there and the fluttering of the curtains was real. This could be quite scary, especially for a little child.

   The right approach these parents could have followed is:

- Accept the child's fears as genuine and give reassurance. When you acknowledge that the shadows look scary, the child is more likely to believe in your reassurance that they are harmless.
- To make the child feel safe, you can close the windows and draw the curtains. So, neither will the curtains flutter nor will the shadows form.
- Sit on the child's bed and hold hands till she dozes off. After a few days the child will gain confidence and all you would need is to tuck her up and leave the room.
- A night lamp helps most children.
- If there's an interconnecting door, leave it ajar.

- The child also may feel happy and relaxed with familiar toys and dolls sharing her bed.

Children will have fears. But as parents, it is your job to help them overcome their fright. Similar steps, based on our common sense, can be taken to help children overcome other fears. Parents must teach them that there is nothing wrong in being scared or feeling nervous and that it is possible to master fears.

When to seek professional help

- If your child's fears are inappropriate for their age
- If the fears have persisted for a long time
- If your child regresses to previously outgrown fears
- If the child is so terrified that he refuses to go to school, is unable to sleep or doesn't let the parents out of sight

15

THE CONCEPT OF UNIQUENESS

Uniqueness in response is manifested by even very young babies. While the slightest sound or bright light may startle some babies, others may not show any response. Thus, conditions that one baby can tolerate may be quite upsetting for another. This tendency to react differently to similar stimuli is carried forward from infancy to adulthood and explains why similar stress factors evoke different reactions in different individuals.

The best way to bring up children is to love them for what they are and not what anyone thinks they ought to be. In this world, no two human beings are exactly alike; even identical twins behave differently in spite of the apparent similarity in genetic endowment. Every child, in some respects, is like all other children, but in some, he is like no other. All children will have many common characteristics but also some unique traits. Understanding and respecting the uniqueness of each child is the key to success.

Some children are highly organized, meticulous and confident, while others are extremely disorganized, negligent and timid. The first group is able to cope with the stress of examinations, stage performance and the like, with consummate ease. The other group is unable to face even minor stresses. Thus, during an examination, they may become so tense that they make a mess of even those questions to which they know the answers by heart. This second group needs careful handling and emotional backing. A comprehensive support system should be developed and deployed for them in such a manner that they don't feel helpless and are able to face various challenges with a positive frame of mind.

If parents keep the concept of uniqueness in mind, many problems arising out of unwarranted and unjustified comparisons among children can be avoided. Undue comparisons have the potential to damage a child's personality—seriously and permanently. Without even realizing it, parents can make a child feel inferior and unwanted by praising his siblings or peers. This is especially damaging if it is done in the background of constant criticism and running down of the child.

Parents cite the example of children who are good in studies or successful in sports, in the fond hope that their children will also be motivated to perform better. If this is done judiciously and skilfully, it might help the child, but insensitivity on the part of parents can injure the child's pride and give him an inferiority complex. As a consequence, instead of improving, the performance of the child deteriorates.

Why do some children fail in spite of having the potential and favourable conditions, while others surmount all adversities to succeed? It is apparent that the strengths and protective factors in their physical, temperamental and psychological make-up drive these children to attain success. These children seem to be remarkably resilient and are able to triumph over adverse circumstances in ways which can surprise us.

Charlie Chaplin had to be twice put in a workhouse due to the poor financial condition of his single mother. He overcame the emotional trauma to become a successful actor. It seems he used his own self-esteem problems to his advantage by playing 'the tramp'.

All children have different needs. Even with twins, one child will have to be fed first—his needs will take priority over the other child who is more patient and, thus, has to wait. Later on, the impatient one may have strong likes and dislikes while the other one continues to be happy with whatever he gets. This is an undesirable situation because the demanding child has his wishes fulfilled and the other one is left out. Parents must cater to the needs of the undemanding child also, so that he doesn't, in any way, feel less cared for. One child will express his views, thoughts and preferences freely; the other one may be introverted and quiet. At mealtime or other similar occasions, parents should create opportunities and persuade the quiet one to speak. They can ask direct questions and may even have to ask the talkative one to simply shut up.

Parents face an eternal dilemma at the dining table because usually what one child likes, the other hates. Ladies' finger is probably the only vegetable uniformly liked by all children. Our elder daughter likes them split vertically while the younger one wants to have small chopped pieces. If both your children are equally doughty and evenly matched in spirit and physique, you will have a harrowing time deciding the menu. But then it was your very own decision to have two children!

It is now well established that a sense of uniqueness builds self-esteem. Parents must understand that uniqueness and high self-esteem are interconnected as well as interdependent. If they can make a child feel unique and special, they have scored a major victory.

To develop a sense of uniqueness, children need to know there is something special about them and that others also think the same. They need to know and do things that no one else can do. If children are given opportunities to use their imagination and creativity and are allowed to express themselves in their own way, they will develop a higher self-esteem.

Those children who feel good about their personal characteristics gain confidence and approach things more positively. These children start making efforts to improve their lot and also succeed at receiving approval and respect from others for their achievements.

When a child starts appreciating his own capabilities and learns to enjoy being different, he becomes destined for glory. Therefore, parents should train themselves to recognize their children's unique abilities and talents. They could do so by following the six steps given below.

Six steps to build your child's sense of uniqueness

1. Accept Your Child

Accepting the child—all of him, including the good and the bad—is the first step towards acknowledging that every child is unique. While parents may focus on changing undesirable behaviour traits, they should not insist upon changing everything about the child to fit their specifications.

It is important that you communicate acceptance of your children by appreciating their assets and praising their accomplishments. You must provide children opportunities to explain their feelings, attitudes, opinions and actions. This can clear many doubts and misunderstandings between parents and children. Remember: Acceptance of uniqueness is the key to self-esteem.

2. Point out the Potential

Parents must point out to children things about them that are different or special. If you discover that your daughter sings well, tell her about her gift and try to nurture her talent. Similarly, children may be gifted at chess, computers, mathematics, tennis or cricket. They can develop their unique talents into extremely profitable careers, provided they receive proper guidance and necessary assistance from their parents.

3. Let Children Do Things Their Own Way

Most parents force their child into using the right hand when they see that he is writing with the left one. Wrong beliefs and taboos are responsible for this practice. By inducing a natural left-hander into becoming a right-hander, parents only end up confusing the child and his brain.

Each child has a different way of doing things. Ankita, 11, always preferred to take medicines in the form of tablets. Even when she was a 3-year-old, she would easily swallow pills of various sizes. Her elder sister, Aparajita, 13, still chokes at the sight of any tablet. She must have medicines as syrups, which have to be given in large quantities because she weighs more than 40 kg.

The message is clear: Don't tamper with the child's basic

temperament. Personality traits need modification only if they are likely to harm the child's future prospects.

4. Allow Children to Express Themselves Creatively

Due to a variety of reasons, some children have a low sense of uniqueness. They often say that they are not good at anything or they can't achieve any success.

Parents should not take these statements lightly as they denote that the child is facing serious problems with his self-esteem. Before these feelings blow-up into a full-grown inferiority complex, they should try to identify areas in which the child has a special interest. If the child can paint, arrange flowers, sing or play an instrument, he should be motivated to take these up as hobbies. At the same time, parents should bolster the child's sense of uniqueness by praising his work.

5. Treat Each Child as an Individual

There are umpteen number of parents whose two kids are exactly opposite in all respects. They have inherited the same set of genes which interact with the same environmental set-up. Then why this difference?

Take the case of Jatin and Nitin at Mr and Mrs Bhandari's household.

'Since he was about 3, everything to do with Jatin has been a struggle,' recalls Mrs Bhandari. 'When it's study time, he throws a tantrum; when it's dinner time, he suddenly loses his appetite; and when it's party time, he fails to find a single good piece of clothing.'

She further adds that Jatin never misses any chance. 'If he felt his younger brother, Nitin, got a bigger piece of chocolate, he would go to the extent of measuring it with a scale. According to him, his teachers are always nicer to his classmates than to him. He is on a constant vigil for any injustice meted out to him, no matter how slight or unintentional. Nitin on the other hand, is as easy to care for as Jatin is difficult. He is organized, self-sufficient, responsible and helpful. Unlike Jatin, he doesn't need constant reminders for bathing, having breakfast, completing homework, etc.'

Mrs Bhandari says, 'I sometimes think, do I love Nitin more? I blame myself for not being a better mother, more appreciative of and responsive to the needs of Jatin. Many times I have promised myself, I will never yell at Jatin like a mad person again; I'll try to remain calm. But moments later, I am hollering at him using both my lungs to the fullest.'

Many parents face a similar predicament, but there is no need to feel guilty or miserable. It has been postulated that even subtle differences in gene patterns can cause major behavioural differences. Keeping this fact in mind, parents should prepare themselves to find apples and oranges growing on the same tree. If parents treat apples as apples and enjoy oranges for being oranges, they will harvest a successful crop.

You should love your children with passion, each for very different reasons. If you have one easy-going child, you should feel happy for the little mercies God bestows. The other more difficult one has been sent to you lest you develop a misguided belief: 'Parenting isn't so hard after all'.

6. Facilitate Your Child's Learning Style

Some children put on music when they are studying; others want pin-drop silence. Some get up early in the morning, while others study late into the night. Parents must identify and support the child's style of learning, provided it is producing the desired results. Trying to alter a child's way of learning may adversely affect his academic performance.

We have seen parents asking/forcing the child to read quietly, while he prefers to read aloud and can remember the facts better by this method. Parents should understand that these children need both visual and auditory inputs to memorize things.

16

PARENTING WITHOUT SHOUTING

Shouting at your children to obey you is like using a horn to move buffaloes off the road—it produces no result. Shouting at one's children may contravene all good parenting slogans, but rest assured, every parent does it and agrees that it doesn't work. Family life is such a cauldron of emotions that you have to be a saint to eschew the urge to shout. But then saints don't marry, rear children and raise families.

Is shouting at one's children the ultimate parental taboo? Should parents be censored unequivocally for shouting at their wards? Many people don't seem to think so.

'When angry, count to four; when very angry, swear,' said writer Mark Twain. And almost all shouters apparently agree that a good yell can clear the air and be liberating and rejuvenating. They sincerely believe that children have to be yelled at to make them tough. Their argument is: 'We don't want our children to be fragile flowers who will wilt the moment heat is turned on.'

You shout at your kids not because you think it is the best option, but because you feel drained, dominated, exploited, criticized and even humiliated. The stress and strain of modern living takes a heavy toll and parents are perpetually on the verge of blowing their fuse. A final act of indiscretion on the part of the child brings about an untimely explosion.

No one would advocate shouting as desirable parental behaviour, but it must be remembered that parenting is not a popularity contest which has to be won at any cost. Parents have to instil right values, teach proper behaviour and educate their children. This is not an easy task and, at times, their patience will be tested to its limits. If you're driven up the wall, shout, but do consider whether you could have managed the situation without exercising your lungs too much. The trick is to shout effectively and judiciously.

Shouting at children when they are out of control indirectly means that you have also lost control over your emotions. While an occasional outburst is acceptable, shouting without remission, especially if the parent-child relationship lacks in mutual love, can be devastating for the child's personality. Shouting is often accompanied by a sound thrashing. Physical punishment must be avoided, as it is fraught with dangers and few, if any, would recommend it.

According to a study by psychiatrists at a hospital affiliated to Harvard Medical School, shouting at children can significantly and permanently alter the structure of their brains.[1] These findings are scary if not downright terrifying, but further research is required to substantiate these early results.

Before you start worrying that shouting at your children will damage their brains and prior to your getting their brains scanned, let us give you good news! Most children quickly become desensitized to excessive parental ranting and simply tune out. Children of loud parents develop a technique of

---

[1]Karpf, A. (2001, March 21). Loud but not proud. *The Guardian*. Retrieved from https://www.theguardian.com/education/2001/mar/21/schools.family andrelationships

'downing their shutters' or 'switching off their receiving sets' the moment their parental radio station starts its daily broadcast. So, is it the parents who suffer more from their shouting than their children?

A permanent damage that relentless shouting can inflict is that these children become pretty adept shouters themselves and develop volatile personalities. The age of the child is also very important in this context. A young child doesn't understand the difference between shouting and hating and may take parental outbursts for hate and dislike for him. With a teenager it is different as he is in a better position to internally reason that your shouting is merely a manifestation of your temporary anguish and, in reality, you love him a lot.

Mrs Neelima Mehra, a working mother, says: 'I shout most at the end of a day, when I am tired or when I have an unusually long list of things to squeeze into an already crowded schedule. I also roar when my children encroach upon the last vestiges of my personal time and space.' The triggers are many and varied but stress and exhaustion come high on the list. It is possible that conditions such as low blood sugar levels may have something to do with the high incidences of shouting.

Shouting provokes a conflict in the minds of most parents. The turmoil of loving and hating the child at the same time becomes difficult for them to handle. When the realities and disappointments of parenting shatter the dreams of becoming an ideal parent, anxiety and guilt are the net result.

The dilemma regarding whether to shout or not, has no simple solution. Parents feel guilty if they shout and frustrated when they suppress the urge. Some shouters put themselves at par with convicted criminals, which in our opinion, is an extreme example of self-flagellation.

Five steps to rest your vocal cords

1. Evolve a suitable disciplinary model for your family and stick to it.
2. If your child is upset, angry or frustrated, avoid getting caught in his foul mood. Refrain from picking up an unnecessary argument, as it is likely to lead to an entirely avoidable shouting match.
3. Think for a while—are you overdoing it? If yes, there is no harm in shutting up and making truce with your child.
4. Evening meals can be used to facilitate communication between the warring parties. However, beware that better communication is not synonymous with 'sermonizing'. Avoid lecturing the child at the dining table; instead, listen to his point of view.
5. If shouting is inevitable, it is better to keep things simple and to speak honestly, without being melodramatic. If you tell the child, 'You have made me very angry', it will have a more positive impact than calling him a horrible brat or an idiot.

17

THE FIGHT TO FEED

Childhood nutrition has always been a subject of much discussion and research. It is one of the most contentious issues in practically all households. The daughter-in-law and the mother-in-law are sometimes at loggerheads as to what is good for the child and what isn't. A decade or two back, the mother-in-law usually prevailed by citing her experience. But that advantage is no more there, thanks to several good books on child rearing and of course the information freely available on the Internet. Equipped with this knowledge, the daughter-in-law feels that she is better qualified in the matters related to child-feeding. This may be true to some extent, but totally dismissing the age-old traditions and child-rearing practices is fraught with danger. Overdependence on the Internet may not only compromise the child's feeding, it may also make the mother anxious and hyper if the child's intake does not match the recommendations of the so-called experts online.

Phew! Did that confuse you? Well that wasn't the intention. All we want is that you strike a balance between the age-old wisdom and the newer child-feeding practices. A harmony between tradition and modernity is advisable as you are likely to get the best results if you combine both.

Children are small but their nutritional needs are big.

They require more nutrition in relation to their size, to fulfil their demands for growth, body maintenance and physical activity. If adequate calories are not available, their growth falters and they become lethargic. According to studies by the United Nations Development Programme (UNDP), 45–55 per cent children receive an inadequate diet. In India, 70 per cent children consume lesser calories per day than the Recommended Dietary Allowance (RDA), the percentage varying in different age groups. Forty-three per cent children in India are underweight, an indication of lesser calorie consumption.

The nutritional requirement of each child varies and is governed by genetic and metabolic differences. The usual parental lament that their child's diet is very little as compared to other children must be explained in light of the above fact. The basic goals in childhood nutrition are achievement of satisfactory growth and avoidance of deficiency states. Good nutrition helps to prevent acute and chronic illness, to develop physical and mental potential and to provide reserves for periods of stress.

Tips to make your child eat right

Many parents are worried about their child's total lack of interest in eating anything nutritionists would consider 'healthy food'. And of course, things have become more complicated due to the easy availability of fast food/junk food these days. Here are some tips to make your child get maximum nutrition with minimum struggle:

1. Milk Is Important

Milk is important for the growth of a child. In fact, it is called a 'complete food' because it contains almost all essential nutrients required to grow optimally. So, many parents battle their children every day to make them drink sufficient quantities of milk, without realizing that the same nutritional benefits can be provided to them through milk hidden in kheer, cereals, custard and puddings. Do you know that a cup of low-fat yoghurt or a slice of cheese has the same amount of calcium as a glass of milk? It is not necessary that your children get their calcium from milk. Instead of battling them to drink milk, offer them yoghurt and cheese, which they will surely eat.

Scientific research has shown that lactase (the enzyme essential for proper digestion of milk) may be present in sub-optimal quantities in certain children. These children develop abdominal colic, bloating or belching on consumption of milk. If your child frequently complains of nausea or vomits after drinking a glass of milk, he may be lactase-deficient. Reduce the quantity of milk to no more than one cup at a time. Alternatively, try giving milk in the form of curd, cheese, etc.

2. Vegetables Are Needed

Rare is the child who never declares an aversion to vegetables. 'My daughter picked them off her plate and lined them up on the dining table to make a point', declared Amita Sharma, at the consultation chamber. This was the net result of the advice to add vegetables to noodles, her daughter Mini's staple diet.

Children like very few vegetables, like ladies' finger or potatoes. You immediately fall into the category of a lucky parent if your child likes fruits, because they provide many of the same vitamins and minerals as vegetables. Juices count, too, but you should vary offerings and serve 100 per cent pure fruit juice. Since too much juice can decrease appetite and cause diarrhoea, serve no more than 250 ml a day.

You have hit the jackpot if your child likes soups! The possibilities are enormous and you can put practically any vegetable in it. Grate the vegetables finely or, even better, mash them up to an unrecognizable state. Ignorance is bliss! Even children who abhor vegetables may consume them in soup version. Many children add sauce to whatever they eat. You can add pureed vegetables to the bottle of tomato sauce kept permanently on your dining table.

3. Fast Food Is a Problem

Pizza, french fries, burgers, noodles, rolls and a variety of fried foods have become the staple diet of most children. Moreover, most kids love deep-fried food. The problem is that fast foods are mostly starch, fat and salt. Like adults, kids over 3 should get no more than 30 per cent of their daily calories from fat.

One method to balance their dietary fat is to use only skimmed milk and low-fat cheese. Prepare a bowl of cut-up fruits—like orange sections and apple slices—before dinnertime. Munching on these makes kids less likely to gorge on greasy foods later. More healthy versions of fast foods can also be made, for example, oven-fried chicken, pizza with low-fat mozzarella cheese, microwave popcorn, etc.

4. Sweets Should Be Restricted

Nimmi loves chocolates, candies, ice cream, shakes, biscuits—for that matter, even plain sugar. Her mother tried to ban sweets, which resulted in devouring of the same by Nimmi on the sly. A ban is not going to work if the fridge and cupboards in the house are loaded with sweets. A ban would only make sweets more desirable. Forbidding a thing is not the solution.

Allowing an occasional chocolate or ice cream will reduce the craving and result in decreased consumption of sweets. Parents and other family members must set an example by eating sweets in moderation.

5. Snacking Must Be Controlled

Many children prefer intermittent snacking to regimented meal hours. If not controlled, the 'snackers' will eventually become 'meal skippers'. Although snacks are important, since most kids cannot go from lunch to dinner without them, skipping meals will deny them a balanced diet. Gross snacking will result in deficiency of vitamins and minerals, and overloading of calories will make them overweight. (Weight management is all about balancing between calories in and calories out).

You shouldn't make children give up snacking; instead, provide them low-fat, low-calorie items, say of hundred calories or less. A child could choose up to one snack before lunch, two between lunch and dinner, and one after dinner.

The best way to make kids eat right is to have healthy foods available at home. For this, a basic knowledge of the nutritional profile of common food items is essential. If you eat right, your children probably will end up eating right, too.

6. Role of Appetite Stimulants

Loss of appetite occurs as the first symptom of almost all diseases. Throat infection (tonsillitis, pharyngitis), oral ulcers, ear infection, viral infections, measles, mumps, gastritis, urinary infection, etc. lead to acute anorexia in children.

Opinion regarding use of drugs to stimulate appetite in children is divided. Some doctors use them; others don't. The main argument against using appetite stimulants is that the effect is temporary. As soon as the drug is stopped, the appetite is lost again. Moreover, no drug is without side effects.

The most commonly prescribed appetite stimulant is Cyproheptadine. It was introduced in the market as an anti-allergic drug. Later, it was found that patients on Cyprohepatadine developed voracious appetites. This drug also causes intense sedation.

Buclizine hydrochloride, available as Longifene, is another commonly used appetite stimulant. Syrups containing Tricholine citrate and Sorbitol solution are also known to stimulate appetite. Tonics containing multivitamins, minerals and iron may also help. Besides these, several Ayurvedic preparations are claimed to improve appetite.

18

SPEECH DELAY

Several parents consult their child's doctor with the refrain that their child has not started to speak even though he is almost 2 years old. When they see other children of the same age speaking coherently they start to panic, assuming that there is something wrong with their child. Mostly this turns out to be a false alarm and soon their child starts talking as well as other children. Before we dwell on the issue of delayed speech, we should know something about the normal development of speech. Since meaningful speech is dependent upon adequate hearing, early assessment of gross hearing in infancy (by 6 months) should be a part of the examination of the child. Do it yourself or ask your paediatrician to perform it.

Development of speech

The earliest indicators of the capability to phonate are seen between 3 to 6 months of age when the baby sometimes laughs out loud or chuckles. He may also make babbling sounds. Between 6 to 9 months, the child makes sounds like 'da-da', 'ba-ba', 'ma-ma'. It is vitally important that the babbling and syllabic repetitions the infant makes be reinforced by imitations from the adults in the family. A reflex speech pattern is established early and communication is enhanced. If a baby says 'da-da' and no one responds with a smile and a 'da-da', the baby may stop saying it and remain silent for lack of a reward.

It is important to know that language includes both expressive (speech) and receptive (understanding) functions. Between 9 to 12 months a child knows his own name and pays attention to simple commands such as 'no' and 'give it to me'. He can copy sounds such as coughing. Between 12 to 15 months the child understands more of what is being told to him. He starts speaking in jargon, with some intelligible words. At this age, children start experimenting with language; they speak unintelligible words, with the voice going up and down as if speaking (jargoning). To outsiders this appears absurd and funny, but parents may be able to comprehend what the child is trying to communicate.

Around 18 months, the child repeats simple words and may have a vocabulary of ten to fifteen words. He uses words such as 'I', 'me' and 'your'. The vocabulary rapidly increases to hundred or more words at 2 years. Language development occurs most rapidly between 2 and 5 years of age. Vocabulary increases from hundred words to more than two thousand. As a rule of thumb, between ages 2 and 5, the number of words in a typical sentence equals the child's age (two by 2 years; three by 3 years; and so on). By 4, the child knows his full name, age and sex. He is able to repeat numbers, rhymes and can count from one to ten. He can also use the past tense. By 5, he is able to use the future tense.

Common causes of speech delay

Some children speak early and some, late; but if a child has no meaningful speech even after 2 years of age then it must be investigated thoroughly. It has been observed that speech development is both earlier and faster in girls. It seems, once they learn to speak, there is no stopping them.

Speech delay is generally due to either the inability to hear or a deficient environmental input.

1. Inability to Hear

Meaningful speech is dependent upon adequate hearing. If things seem amiss, an exhaustive evaluation of the auditory apparatus must be made, as development of speech relies heavily on the ability to hear. Lack of early speech beyond the babbling sounds in the first 3 to 6 months, usually means a sensorineural defect (inner-ear, cochlear or auditory nerve malfunction). I know of a case where the parents first noticed that their 6-month-old child was not responding to the loud noise of firecrackers on Diwali night. The grandma declared him to be extremely brave, but the mother was not convinced. She brought the child for examination and it was found that the child was having a severe hearing defect. On history taking, it was found that the mother was administered Gentamycin injections during pregnancy, which presumably was the cause of deafness in the child. Timely detection and early intervention in the form of a hearing aid initially, and a cochlear implant later, has helped the child to develop near normal speech.

2. Deficient Environmental Input

Development of linguistic skills (speech) depends mainly on environmental input. The more the parents and other adults in the family (grandparents, etc.) talk to the child, the faster the development of speech. Unfortunately, the advent of nuclear families, especially where both parents are working, deprives children of this much-needed auditory input. On top of it, the idiot-box takes away most of the evening when the parents could have talked to the child. It is a universal phenomenon seen across the globe where a small child is made to watch TV because the parents themselves are parked in front of it.

Let us make it very clear—a young child cannot learn language by watching TV. The child only watches the pictures without really concentrating on the dialogues. So, if you want your child to speak, switch off the idiot box and talk to him. Tell him stories, read to him from picture books, sing in his ears. Picture books have a special role in the development of verbal language. Parents should have lots of picture books (storybooks with minimal text and plenty of pictures) at home. They should read the story while pointing out to the pictures in the book. It is not necessary to stick to the story written in the book. You can use your imagination and make up new stories to get the child involved. Reading aloud and showing pictures provides the child with double stimulation—auditory as well as visual. This double input will lead to faster acquisition of language.

Once the child has developed a basic vocabulary, focus his attention on a particular picture and request a response (by asking, 'What's that?'), and then give the child feedback ('Right! It's a cat'). This question-feedback routine should be repeated many times in the course of reading a book. As the child's vocabulary grows, parents can ask more complex questions, requesting descriptions ('What colour is the cat? What's that cat doing?'). Such sessions involving active participation of the child, immediate feedback by the parent, repetition and gradual enhancement of difficulty are ideal for learning a language.

3. *Miscellaneous Causes*

- **Mental retardation:** Language is a critical measure of both cognitive and emotional development. Any factor which adversely affects the growth of the brain (during the intrauterine period or at the time of birth) can lead to delayed speech development. In fact, non-development of speech by 2 years may be the first indication that the child is suffering from mental retardation.

- **Child abuse and neglect (CAN):** These are correlated with delayed language, particularly the ability to convey emotions. Abused and neglected children suffer from deficient environmental input (lack of parental interaction), which adversely affects their speech development.

- **Multilingualism:** This, as a cause of delayed speech, has many takers. For example, a Tamilian family with a young child gets relocated from the south of India to the north. The child is faced with a vernacular language (Tamil) at home, Hindi amongst his playmates and English at school. Coping with three different languages may confuse the growing brain of the small child, leading to delay in development of speech. However, in most instances, after a while the brain is able to sort out these confusing signals and the child develops mastery over all the three languages.

19

THE IMPACT OF GADGETS AND GIZMOS

Of all the gadgets and gizmos, mobile phones have undoubtedly had the biggest impact on our lifestyles. The way we think, eat, sleep, behave and socialize, all have been transformed by this small, palm-held device. Add to this the ubiquitous laptops, Bluetooth devices, tablets, gaming consoles and not the least, TV—and the frightening picture of a society trapped in a prison of its own making is complete. The explosion of digital technology combined with the exponential growth of social media has forced us to start living in a make-believe world.

These gadgets and gizmos have become a source of constant conflict between parents and children. Thanks to them, family time has become severely compromised and may soon disappear totally. Making children go to bed at an appropriate time, eat at designated hours and study regularly have all become herculean tasks for parents.

Anila, 11, used to be an intelligent, carefree child. One evening she happened to watch a horror show on her smartphone which greatly terrified her. She started to get nightmares and would wake up from her sleep, shouting in terror. She also began to stammer and wet the bed. In her next exams, she failed in two subjects.

Divyansh, 4, has linguistic delay. Saniya, 7, can't see without her spectacles. Chetan, 9, is an overweight, overwrought, recluse. Tony, 12, is violent, hyperactive and has learning difficulties. Vineet, 15, has been recently diagnosed as diabetic. All of them were highly dependent on their gadgets.

These children merely constitute the tip of the iceberg when it comes to health problems related to gadgets and gizmos. Several researches have highlighted harmful effects of the excessive use of these devices on the health of children. This is especially true when the addiction starts at a young age.

Health hazards of excessive use of gadgets and gizmos

1. *Obesity*: It has been observed that prevalence of obesity increases by 2 per cent for every hour of using these devices. Altered levels of the hormones leptin and ghrelin boost appetite and lead to increase in body fat. These children remain largely inactive, therefore their BMR (Basal Metabolic Rate) goes down and they are unable to burn the calories they consume. Due to lack of physical activity, their blood cholesterol levels also increase. There is no denying the fact that the overuse of gadgets is responsible for the ongoing obesity epidemic in children. An obese child is likely to develop hypertension, heart disease, arthritis and back pain later in life.

2. *Diabetes*: Gadgets-cued eating, which is generally in the form of unhealthy, calorie-dense snacks, has played havoc with the health of children. Gadgets severely compromise the time children can spend playing outdoors. This lack of physical activity, combined with the habit of skipping meals and heavy snacking, leads to excessive weight gain

and subsequent development of diabetes (Type 2 diabetes mellitus).

3. *Sleep Disorders*: Light from the screen of these devices suppresses the production of melatonin. This hormone is intricately involved in the human sleep cycle. Disturbance in melatonin secretion causes lack of sleep. The child remains awake and spends more time with the gadgets, leading to further suppression of this hormone. Thus, a vicious cycle sets in and the normal sleep cycle is totally disrupted.

4. *Growth Retardation*: It is a well-established fact that the growth hormone is produced during surges in sleep and during vigorous exercise. As the child is neither sleeping well nor exercising, the secretion of this hormone gets suppressed and the growth of the child gets affected.

5. *Lack of Creativity*: Every hour that is wasted on using these gadgets could have been utilized for physical and mental self-improvement. Children who are always playing with gadgets and gizmos lack originality, newness and imagination. When we went to judge a story-writing competition at a school, we were stunned to find that most of the students had submitted stories based on movies/ TV serials with minor variations.

6. *Poor Concentration*: The development of brain cells that govern attention span is impaired in gadget-addicts. This not only leads to a short attention span, but also causes nervousness, excitability and antisocial behaviour. Poor intellectual stimulation in chronic gadget users, especially while they are young, leads to reading difficulties. This later translates into poor academic performance and underachievement. These children also have a poor self-

image and may suffer from inferiority complex.

7. **Autism**: This condition may develop in prolific gadgets and gizmo users, who deprive themselves of social interaction and have poor social skills. They remain confined in their world, are not able to communicate well and generally fail in interpersonal relationships.

8. **Poor Immune System**: It has been seen that the unhealthy lifestyle of these children compromises their immune system, making them more susceptible to a variety of disorders. The radiation emitted by these devices have been linked to changes in the mast cells (immune cells) of the skin. Disrupted hormones increase the chances of mutations in cell DNA. These mutations, along with an altered immune response, make them more prone to develop cancer.

9. **Premature Puberty**: Hormonal imbalance is frequently observed in children who use gadgets for prolonged periods. A low level of melatonin seen in these children is responsible for the premature onset of puberty.

10. **Headache and Migraine**: Continuous use of gadgets causes eye strain. These children suffer from lack of sleep and brain fatigue. All these can precipitate headaches and attacks of migraine.

11. **Short-sightedness**: Staring at the screen for hours together can lead to eye damage. This is probably the most important contributing factor for the increasing incidence of short-sightedness, or myopia, in young children.

12. **Linguistic Delay**: Several parents complain that their child has not started to speak even after 3 years of age. If both mother and father are working and the family spends the entire evening in front of the TV, speech delay in the child

is hardly surprising. Young children are attracted to fast-moving pictures during the airing of advertisements. They lose interest the moment the slow-moving serials with dawdling dialogues start. Remember: Children cannot learn a language by merely watching TV! They need the stimulating company of their parents, who should never let any opportunity to communicate with their children go a-begging. Reading stories from brightly coloured picture books is a sure method of developing linguistic skills of your child.

13. *Epilepsy*: Certain forms of epileptic fits are precipitated by bright, flickering lights. Sleep deprivation and fatigue caused by endless hours of focusing on the screens of gadgets is an important provoking factor.

14. *Alzheimer's Disease*: It has been observed that additional daily hours of TV-viewing increases the risk of Alzheimer's.

So, what's the way out?

Endless TV viewing, excessive use of mobile phones and playing on a gaming console by children have become a big menace, especially if both parents are working and there is no one with authority to supervise them. Here are some tips to control this:

- Regarding TV viewing, sit down with your child and select ten programmes appropriate for the child's age yourself, but let the child put tick marks on them. This way the child will feel that he is taking his own important decisions. It should be clearly told to the child that he can watch only those ten programmes per week. However, an extra programme or two on weekends may be permitted if the child is otherwise conforming to what is expected of him academically and socially.

- Mobile phone addiction is a huge menace. One recent study reported that Indian college students check their phones up to 150 times a day.[2] Most of this time is usually wasted on excessive messaging, video chatting, watching web series and movies, thereby leading to a lack of productiveness.

- Parents of young children themselves are partly responsible for inducing mobile phone addiction in their children. Whenever they are busy they let the child play with the phone. Gradually the child starts demanding the phone more and more. Parents should delay providing phone to the child as long as possible. Older children who have to attend coaching etc. may be provided mobile phones, but with proper monitoring.

- As far as laptop use and the habit of playing on a gaming console is concerned, parents have to keep a close watch on the time spent by the child on these devices. Children should be motivated to spend more time playing outdoor games rather than becoming couch potatoes. If parents themselves are outdoor people it's easier for them to stimulate children to get involved in such activities. A fair number of adolescents are becoming health-conscious and hitting the gym seems to be the new fad amongst youth. Keeping in

[2]Agha, E. (2018, April 17). 150 Times a Day: Study Shows Indian Students' Alarming Smartphone Addiction. *News18*. Retrieved from https://www.news18.com/news/india/according-to-new-study-students-check-their-mobile-devices-as-many-as-150-times-in-a-day-1720539.html.

mind the financial aspect, parents can discuss and decide about a gym membership.

These processes teach the child to be selective and make him more responsible. The child also learns self-denial, because, undoubtedly, there will be some programmes he would like to watch but not as much as others. This helps to establish judgment and values within the child. Rationalization of the use of gadgets and gizmos will make the child more communicative, productive, affectionate, relaxed, morally responsible and socially acceptable.

The fact remains that gadgets and gizmos can't be banished from our lives, but at the same time, you must ensure that they do not begin to rule the life of your child. Let them be a part of your child's daily routine, but do not let them become the most important part.

20

HANDLING A HYPERACTIVE CHILD

Rahul, 8, is an inattentive, impulsive and hyperactive child who is facing serious academic, social and disciplinary problems. He often fails to finish things he starts, doesn't seem to listen and is easily distracted. Because of poor concentration he makes frequent careless mistakes. He often loses books, notebooks, pens and pencils. He has difficulty in staying seated, is fidgety and keeps shifting from one activity to another. He is always running about or climbing things and needs a lot of supervision.

Rahul is suffering from attention deficit hyperactivity disorder (ADHD), which accounts for the largest category of psychological referrals among children. This disorder affects about 5 per cent primary school children, with 75 per cent or more being boys. The exact cause of ADHD is not known but it seems to be a genetic disorder. There is presumptive evidence of minimal brain damage, which, in most cases, is genetically inherited, but could also be due to complications during pregnancy and birth. A history of learning or conduct problems is commonly found in a parent or close relative of children with ADHD. Early identification and prompt intervention is crucial for these children, as it can prevent maladjustment at home and within the peer group.

The problem is that most parents are unaware of this

condition and simply try to control the child's behaviour by punishing him. This can lead to conflict and acrimony between the two parties and worsening of the situation. Minor forms of hyperactive behaviour are seen in many children and parents need not worry too much about it because these children usually settle down with the passage of time. It is the serious type of ADHD that needs expert handling.

Managing a hyperactive child

1. General Principles

Although general principles of managing a hyperactive child are useful, but individualized care for each child achieves greater success. Effective treatment depends upon close cooperation and constant communication between the psychotherapist, parents and school. This helps to reduce frustration and feelings of helplessness in the child, as well as care providers.

- When a hyperactive child acts or behaves impulsively in a socially incorrect manner, don't just point out the mistake but try to explain the inappropriateness of the behaviour to the child. Reinforce proper behaviour immediately through praise or by offering a gift, because waiting too long to reward the child may not achieve the desired effect.
- Initially, hyperactive children should be exposed to small group interactions. Due to better control and less distractions, they are able to accomplish simple tasks and feel successful. This gives them confidence to attempt more difficult academic work.
- Parents and teachers should try to identify strengths of the child that can be publicly announced or praised. This not only boosts the child's morale but also changes the negative

mindset of his peers towards him.

- A hyperactive child finds it difficult to remain seated for an extended period of time. Teachers can arrange to have the child run an errand: Cleaning the blackboard, distributing corrected notebooks, etc. This allows the child to leave the seat for a purposeful activity and generates feelings of importance and accomplishment.

- At home, an alarm clock can be used to deal with the problem of remaining seated. Make a deal with the child to get up only after the alarm goes off. Initially, set the alarm for thirty minutes and subsequently increase it to forty-five minutes or one hour. The anticipation of being allowed to leave the seat motivates the child to remain seated. This conditioning exercise succeeds with most children and should also help your child.

- Hyperactive children are generally disorganized and frequently forget to jot down the homework. They also have problems in listening and taking notes. Parents must establish close cooperation with teachers and request them to spare a few minutes to verify whether the child has completed classwork and taken down the home assignment or not. Occasionally, teachers may provide the child with extra time for completing their work. Help of a friend may also be taken by the parents and the incomplete work can be xeroxed from his/her notebook.

- These children keep their things in a very disorderly manner. They should be helped in arranging the books and notebooks, organizing the study table and cleaning the drawers. Encourage the child to make it a weekly task.

- Designate the study area. Do not allow the child to study in all corners of the house in a haphazard manner. To prevent distraction and improve concentration, put off the room lights and use a table lamp. Treating the study area as sacred (by removing slippers, lighting incense) may help in motivating the child.

- Avoid giving multiple instructions and assignments simultaneously. Allow the child to finish one assignment, before going on to the next one. Some children get flustered by seeing too many problems on the same page. Take a sheet of paper and cover the rest while allowing the child to tackle one problem at a time.

- Permitting the child to use graph paper while doing arithmetic work provides a structured format in which to place numbers. Large graph papers should be used so that the child can easily place one number in each box. This helps the child to approach the task in a systematic manner, and this is generally useful in all ADHD cases. There is no harm in allowing these children to use a calculator. They can also be provided with basic math tables and formulas while doing their assignment. The aim here is to successfully accomplish the task at hand, by avoiding frustration of not being able to remember and recall the facts.

- Some children grasp better if provided with auditory and visual inputs concomitantly. Parents can audio-record a chapter so that the child can read and listen at the same time.

- Computers/laptops are now available in most homes and the child should be familiarized with them at the earliest. Computers can be used to organize the child's work, to teach typing skills and to improve word power by using various software packages readily available in the market. The child will feel good about himself, especially on seeing a report generated by his own efforts. Computers are fascinating and motivating, but also addictive, so take care that the child doesn't spend too much time working/playing on it.

- Organize your child's things at night to avoid stress and confusion before going to school in the morning. Ask the child to develop a checklist, so that the school dress, books, notebooks and home assignments are ready for the next morning. This will help the child to feel secure as he reaches the school better prepared.

- Parents must be realistic about their expectations from the child and should ignore minor incidents and focus on the major areas of concern. They should familiarize themselves with the situations, which are frustrating to the child. Avoiding confrontation and providing emotional support is the right approach during these moments.

2. Psychotherapy

Psychotherapy helps the child to:

- gain self-esteem
- release pent-up frustration
- acquire control over impulsiveness

Psychotherapists use 'behaviour modification' to control hyperactivity and improve the concentration of the child. This mode of treatment involves a system of incentives, deterrents, daily report cards, etc. Some people also recommend family therapy in which all family members are given guidance to deal with the child.

3. Special Diet

In 1973, Dr Benjamin Feingold, a paediatrician, put forward a hypothesis linking hyperactivity to the use of artificial colours and flavours, preservatives and naturally occurring substances in food called salicylates. He postulated that eliminating these substances from the child's diet would result in the remission of the problem. However, subsequent research has failed to substantiate Dr Feingold's dietary theory. The treatment of ADHD by special diets has raised a great deal of controversy and further research in this area is required.

4. Medication

Most commonly used psychostimulants for ADHD are dexedrine and ritalin. These drugs improve concentration and increase a child's awareness of the world around him. More than half the children exhibit a decrease in unwanted symptoms and almost 10 per cent show a dramatic improvement in their behaviour. It should be kept in mind that these drugs don't cure the disorder but alleviate bothersome symptoms. Common side effects seen with these drugs are nausea, loss of appetite and weight loss. There is some concern that use of psychostimulant drugs may lead to drug dependency/abuse, although there is no research to prove this.

5. Role of Fish Oil

The results of a pilot study published in *Nutrition Journal* suggest that children with ADHD can benefit from daily supplementation of high levels of purified fish oils.[3] The eight-week study demonstrated that children who consumed between 8 and 16 g per day of eicosapentaenoic acid (EPA) and

---

[3]Sorgi, P.J., Hallowell, E.M., Hutchins, H.L., & Sears. B. (2007). Effects of an open-label pilot study with high-dose EPA/DHA concentrates on plasma phospholipids and behavior in children with attention deficit hyperactivity disorder. *Nutrition Journal*, 6(1), 16.

docosahexaenoic acid (DHA), the long chain omega-3 fatty acids found in fish oil, showed significant improvements in their behaviour rated by both their parents and the psychiatrist working with them.

The study monitored the ratio of two fatty acids in the blood: Arachidonic acid (AA) and eicosapentaenoic acid (EPA). It is known from previous studies that children with ADHD have a high AA/EPA ratio in the blood compared to controlled children. The amount of purified fish oil for each child was adjusted until his or her AA/EPA ratio reached an ideal level.

The study found a statistically significant improvement in inattention, hyperactivity, oppositional/defiant behaviour and conduct disorders as the AA/EPA ratio in the blood was lowered. The findings were true for children taking their optimal dosage of drugs to manage their ADHD as well as for the children who had voluntarily stopped taking their drugs during the study.

This is an important study as it indicates when adequate levels of fish oils are added to the diet, significant behavioural changes can occur. This study also indicates that the growing epidemic of ADHD may have a strong nutritional component—the lack of sufficient intake of omega-3 fatty acids, such as EPA and DHA. Equally important is that supplementation with high-dose fish oil is synergistic with existing drugs, giving both the physician and parents new dietary approaches towards correcting this growing epidemic in children.

21

BEDWETTING:
A COMMON CHILDHOOD DISORDER

Bedwetting or enuresis is a common childhood problem in which there is an involuntary passage of urine during sleep. It is a frequent cause of emotional turmoil and tension in several homes. Two most common techniques adopted by parents are restricting the child's fluid intake in the evening and making him pass urine before going to bed. But these measures generally don't help much and the child fails to remain dry during the night. Parents losing their cool and scolding the child further complicates matters. Seeing how frequent and troublesome this problem is, we will discuss it in some detail.

Children with the problem of bedwetting suffer from low self-esteem, shame and guilt. Poor school performance and emotional disturbances are commonly seen in these children. They are afraid of being discovered by their peers and often fear being teased and humiliated by their own siblings and relatives. They opt out of social activities. Most bedwetting children will not go to camps or participate in sleepovers with friends.

Children should not be labelled 'bedwetters' unless the

symptom persists beyond the age of 5 years. There is little justification for starting drug treatment before this age as most of the times, the child becomes all right by the time he is 5. Bedwetting occurs more frequently in boys than in girls. It will often have been present in one of the parents, suggesting a hereditary tendency. Scientists have found a genetic marker linked to enuresis.

These children often have a small bladder capacity and are generally deep sleepers. A small or immature bladder is not able to store all the urine that accumulates during the night. It sends a message to the spinal cord saying, 'I am full'. The spinal cord then messages the social awareness part of the brain that knows it is unacceptable to urinate in bed. However, the social awareness part of the brain is deep asleep and unable to respond to the message emanating from the full bladder. The spinal cord does not have any social awareness, so in the absence of the brain's command on what to do, it acts on its own and messages the bladder: 'Empty yourself!'

Two types of bedwetting

1. Persistent type

In this type, the child has never been dry at night. It is often due to faulty toilet training. Both, too strict or too lenient an attitude of parents is harmful. If the parents are very rigid, it may lead to an angry response from the child. The child may unconsciously defy the parents by wetting the bed. On the other hand, if parents are not supportive and sufficiently involved in toilet training, the child will fail to develop good bladder control, leading to his wetting the bed.

2. Regressive type

In this type, a child, who was previously dry, begins to wet the bed at night, after a stressful episode. Move to a new house, marital conflict, sexual abuse, birth of a sibling, death in the family, school-related stress—all are capable of inducing bedwetting. This type of bedwetting is often intermittent and transitory; prognosis is better and management is less difficult than in those children who have never been dry.

A few facts to remember

In both types of bedwetting, generally no physical abnormality is found. A urine examination should be routinely done for all bedwetting children to exclude urinary tract infection (UTI) as a cause. When bedwetting is associated with UTI, treatment promptly cures the problem. These children should also be checked for anomalies of urethra, bladder and ureters, and for diabetes.

Sensitivity to milk, chocolate and citrus juices (orange, pineapple, peach or tomato) have also been linked to bedwetting. If the problem of bedwetting is severe, it may be worthwhile to eliminate milk and milk products (curd, cheese, ice cream) for a week or two. If the bedwetting stops, milk is the culprit. Similarly, the effect of eliminating chocolates and citrus fruits on bedwetting can also be checked out. You will have to eliminate foods to which a child is sensitive for a sufficiently long time before you can see a positive change. In one of our patients, the beneficial effect of stopping citrus juices was evident almost four months later.

Management

Bedwetting is a perplexing problem to manage. The best results are achieved when a child is motivated, there is close cooperation between child, parents and the doctor, and there is no evidence of serious psychiatric problem in the child or family.

General measures

- Rewarding the child for being dry at night is a useful step. The child feels encouraged and is likely to make a sincere effort to avoid passing urine in bed.
- Punishment or humiliation of the child by parents or others is strongly discouraged. The child is likely to lose confidence and may even develop defiance, leading to aggravation of the problem.
- In case of young children, the parents should change the soiled clothes. Older children should be expected to wash the soiled clothes themselves. However, this should not be turned into a prestige issue by the parents.
- Children should be given no liquids after dinnertime.
- The child should be asked to pass urine before going to bed.
- Parents may wake up the child once, to take him to the bathroom, when they are retiring to bed. Waking the child repeatedly to pass urine is not advised as it may provoke anger and resentment in the child.

Urinary bladder training

A 7- to 8-year-old child can be trained to hold his urine. During daytime, ask the child to hold the urine as long as possible, instead of passing it at the first urge. If the child makes a sincere effort and succeeds, reward him for his endeavour. Gradually increase the time interval. Also train him to stop and start the stream a few times during urination. These exercises can stretch his bladder capacity as well as help him develop voluntary control over the sphincter muscle that holds urine in the bladder.

Enuresis alarm

In western countries, various alarm systems are available. These rely on a sensor placed under the sheets, which detects the passage of a small amount of urine and sets off an alarm to wake up the child. Enuresis alarm is a simple, safe and effective device for bedwetting. The principle behind using these alarms is to awaken the children when they are bedwetting, by an external alarm system, until they learn to recognize their own internal signal of bladder fullness while in deep sleep and awaken on their own to empty the bladder.

Drugs

The most effective drug in the treatment of bedwetting is imipramine. This medication, however, has some side effects and should only be used under close medical supervision. Many children start bedwetting again after stopping this drug. Two other drugs, amantadine and oxybutynin, have also been tried with varying degrees of success.

It has been observed that giving 500 mg of magnesium at bedtime allows the bladder to stretch enough to hold the urine overnight.

Recently, an entirely new modality of treatment for bedwetting has become available. This comes in the form of nasal sprays or tablets. Parents can use either one of these. The nasal spray has to be instilled in the nose of the child at bedtime. Tablets are given orally before going off to sleep. These tablets dissolve instantaneously in the mouth and there is no need to give water. They contain desmopressin hormones (minirin, D-void), which reduce urinary output, thus providing quick relief from bedwetting. The cost of this treatment, along with the drug, is around ₹2000 per month. The treatment has to be taken for a minimum of three months.

To summarize, bedwetting is a multi-factorial problem, which requires a multidisciplinary approach. With proper management, the results are generally good. Besides medicines, parental support is of vital importance in the management of this tricky problem.

22

RECURRING ABDOMINAL PAIN, OR RAP

Mrs Neeta Mehta came to the clinic with the following problem:

'My 8-year-old son, Apoorv, keeps complaining of stomach aches. Sometimes the pain is severe, but mostly it is mild. He has undergone check-ups several times but no conclusive diagnosis could be made. Medicines provide temporary relief and he still talks about stomach discomfort and uneasiness. What can be done about it?'

We are reproducing the answer in the form of this write-up. We are sure it will be of help to many parents who have, at some point in time, faced this not-so-uncommon riddle.

Recurrent Abdominal Pain, or RAP, is like rap music—very difficult to understand! You and your doctor may indulge in endless investigations without coming to any diagnosis. However, a basic stool and urine routine and microscopic examination, along with ultrasonography (USG) of the abdomen, should always be carried out in all children having RAP.

If your child is suffering from pain in the abdomen, but otherwise looks well, you can be almost sure that the problem is not serious. Also, if the pain is located around the navel, it is less likely to be dangerous, but if it is in the flanks (either right or left), chances are that it could be something serious. See a doctor if you have cause to be anxious. Some important causes of abdominal pain in children are psychological factors, medical causes and surgical conditions.

Psychological factors

School-going children often complain of recurrent abdominal pain, generally located around the navel. In most cases, the pain is not severe and the child forgets all about it if he is involved in doing something interesting. It rarely wakes the child from sleep and he is perfectly all right in between the attacks, which may last from a few moments to longer, but rarely for more than half an hour. Usually, these children are quite intelligent.

Emotional trauma due to any reason may be the cause of abdominal pain in such children. Is the child being bullied in school? Is the child afraid of a new teacher? Are the examinations causing much anxiety? Is the child upset because of a quarrel between the parents?

It is not always easy to probe the mind of a child. If the symptoms persist, take the advice of a doctor, who may even refer the child to a family counsellor, psychologist or a psychiatrist. Don't upset the child by remarks like, 'You are just acting' or 'Do not try to fool us'. Such children do experience pain, but the symptom is probably related more to the mind rather than the body—possibly a subconscious way of attracting the parents' attention for more body contact. Hence, the treatment lies in understanding the child and helping him overcome the emotional problem, if any.

Medical causes

Although various worm infestations can cause abdominal pain, the tendency to presume that they are the predominant cause in most cases is wrong. Roundworms, threadworms, hookworms and whipworms can be eradicated by administering albendazole or mebendazole. Care must be taken to treat the entire family if worms are found in the stool of any one member. For treating tapeworms, niclosamide and praziquantel are used.

Giardiasis (intestinal infection by giardia lamblia) and amoebiasis (intestinal infection by entamoeba histolytica) may be suspected in children with persistent or recurrent pain in the abdomen. A stool examination of a fresh sample can be taken to confirm the diagnosis. A course of metronidazole will solve the problem in most cases. In some cases, amoeba may invade the liver and cause hepatic amoebiasis. This leads to abdominal discomfort and pain of varying degrees. If treated inadequately, it may lead to a liver abscess. A full course of metronidazole or tinidazole must be administered to cure this condition. Secnidazole and ornidazole can also be tried. In some difficult cases, a long course of chloroquine may be given.

Bacillary dysentery is another important cause of griping pain in the abdomen, along with passage of blood or mucus in the stools, which may not necessarily be loose. This condition can be treated by the use of a wide variety of antibiotics.

Surgical conditions

Medical conditions such as appendicitis, intestinal obstruction, intussusception, strangulated hernia, torsion of testes, all begin with abdominal pain before other signs and symptoms appear. The pain rapidly increases in intensity and if surgical intervention is not done on time, the condition may become life-threatening.

Other common surgical conditions that can cause spasmodic pain in the abdomen is a stone in the urinary tract. The onset of pain in such cases, is sudden. The pain is often located in the back and extends towards the groin. A dull ache persists, with outbursts of shooting, unbearable pain. This may be associated with the passage of blood in the urine. USG can usually clinch the diagnosis. Cystoscopy, laser or conventional surgery may be required for removing the stone, depending upon its site and size.

Finally, we would like parents not to panic when faced with this very common problem. But at the same time, they should remain wary of any persistent abdominal pain, especially if it keeps on increasing in intensity with the passage of time. We know a doctor-couple that almost lost their only son because they didn't think that his abdominal pain was due to a ruptured appendix.

FOUR

ISSUES RELATED TO SCHOOL/ SCHOOLING

PREPARING THE CHILD FOR THE FIRST DAY AT SCHOOL

It's Ritesh's first day at school! The entire Gupta household is reverberating with excitement, anxiety, apprehension and anticipation. Ritesh appears very tense and is crying incessantly since morning. On reaching the school, he clings to his mother tightly and doesn't let go. Any attempt to reason, cajole or persuade him results in even louder wailing.

Ritesh is having acute 'separation anxiety' and is afraid that he may be separated from his parents permanently. Such scenes are a frequent phenomenon, repeated year after year on the first day at school. Separation anxiety, if not handled properly, can lead to school refusal and school phobia.

Few simple measures and some prior preparation can make your child's first day at school a happy one.

- Take your child to the school before the session starts and familiarize him with the surroundings.
- If possible, you can try to introduce the child to his teacher.
- Let the child see the swings and slides in the school playground. They are sure to interest and enthuse the child.

- Tell the child about neighbourhood kids who go to the same school and help the child make friends with them.
- If you plan to send your child by school bus, you should take him on the bus route a few times. Also show the bus stop from where he will board the bus.
- Leave the child occasionally with a friend or a relative for an hour or two. In this way, he will get used to your absence and also learn that separation from you is only temporary.
- Start a 'school-going drill' a few days prior to the opening of school. Make the child sleep and rise early, bathe in the morning and eat breakfast. Gradually, the child will get used to this routine and will not face any difficulty when the school starts.
- If you plan to drop your child to the school, don't linger. Once you have said goodbye, leave promptly.
- While the child may not be allowed to take his favourite toy car/teddy into the classroom, he can certainly keep it safely in his school bag.
- Some children have a favourite blanket or other such items to which they are emotionally attached. Cut a piece of that cloth and keep it in his pocket. The child can touch it and feel comforted when he needs.
- Motivate the child to go to school by describing your own pleasant experiences and memories of school.
- Make it a point to receive your 'VIP' after the school—at least during the initial days.

Don't the above tips appear simple and practical? Well, it's simply common sense.

24

INFLUENCE OF THE PEER GROUP

Parents lay the foundations for social behaviour, teachers modulate it, but it is the peer group which enables the child to develop and practise the skills of cooperation and competition, independence and dependence, and leadership and followership. Thus, interactions with, and acceptance by, peers, constitute a very important stage in the development of a child. Peers may form an important part of the success equation or they may precipitate failure.

Financial status and the ability to possess material basics play an important role in feelings of well-being. Children who are not able to match their peers as per material possessions like trendy clothes, latest bicycles, stylish school bags or water bottles, etc. can get an inferiority complex pertaining to their presumed poverty. Parents must swiftly counter these damaging tendencies by explaining the disadvantages of getting into unnecessary and wasteful competition. However, no child should be denied reasonable requests and, occasionally, some unreasonable ones, too.

Some aggressive children of affluent parents, especially the ones with no worthwhile achievement to their name, try to impress their peers by splurging money. They attract vulnerable children by treating them in fast food joints, taking them to the movies and allowing them to use their jazzy bicycles. Later, they exploit these children by involving them in nefarious and sinful activities. They teach them to drink, smoke, lie and steal, thus, slowly but surely, pushing them on the path of delinquency.

Bullying and teasing in school can have a catastrophic effect on academic performance and life in general. If this menace is not dealt with firmly and in time, it can play havoc with the confidence and self-image of the child. Something as trivial as dark complexion, odd surname, longish nose or thick spectacles can lead to teasing. Bullying—which could sadly also originate from the teaching staff—can cause an inferiority complex which may not easily be overcome even in later life.

Untidiness and unfashionable clothes serve to invite the unwelcome attention of classmates, who target these children as prime objects for making fun. Personality traits like frequent blinking of eyes, stuttering or stammering are a frequent cause of harassment. These children are already vulnerable from a psychological point of view; relentless teasing and bullying can cause severe damage to their psyche.

The significance of unkindness and cruelty should never be underestimated and a child's perception of it, never scorned. Teachers and parents must act in tandem to protect the child from this scourge. They should keep an eye on a child's behaviour and should remain especially vigilant for the signs of anxiety and apprehension. Peer group activities of the child must be monitored discreetly and all possible communication channels utilized to help the child. If properly planned intervention is delayed, the child's personality development may be seriously undermined. Timidity and delinquency are natural corollaries of personality derangement.

Danish, a Class 10 student, was average in studies but very good in sports. He was the eldest of four children in the household, which also included his aged grandparents. His father, a clerk in a government office, somehow managed to make the ends meet.

During the annual sports meet, Danish won the 'Best Athlete' award. He was befriended by some well-to-do senior boys of the school and they soon became a close group which could be seen huddled together in all corners of the school. Danish started smoking and bunking classes for going to movies and restaurants with his group. He and his friends were frequent visitors to the expensive discotheques of the city. Danish was amazed and dazed by the endless supply of cash his friends had.

This continued throughout the year, at the end of which Danish was debarred from appearing in the board examinations, because his attendance fell short of the required minimum. Out of anxiety and apprehension, he kept this hidden from his father. During the examination days he used to go out of the house on the pretext of appearing for the exams and returned with the examination paper acquired from one of his friends. On the day of the result, he committed suicide.

It is extremely difficult to identify, quantify and evaluate exactly what went wrong and where. What are the hereditary-environmental variables which combine to distort and blight a child's personal-social growth? What makes some children play truant at school or become juvenile delinquents, while others become model students and responsible citizens?

To 'search' for the cause, we will have to first open the 'home page'. A faulty home environment may be the reason for a child's maladjustment at school. Further searches must be made at the school site, where the child may be rejected and harassed by teachers and classmates. Afraid, bored, confused, prejudiced, abused and inappropriately taught, the child falls short of expected standards and is promptly labelled as a failure.

Our education system brutally rejects those who fall short of the supposed norms. Rejection and failure in school may generate vicious hatred and revolt within the child, against a system that seems to exist to frustrate him. It is too clear today that the number of these thwarted, rejected and angry young people is on the increase, to the great detriment of themselves and society. This, in fact, is a failure on the part of the 'schools' to meet the intellectual and psychological needs of such children.

Optimum harmony between the school and home, results in maximum benefits for the child. A close involvement of the parents in the schooling of their child is of utmost importance if the child has to rise above the ordinary. Parent-teacher meetings are significant opportunities through which teachers can interact simultaneously with the parents and child. These occasions must be utilized not only to discuss the present performance but also to plan for the future. If a child's weaknesses and problem areas are being highlighted, remedial measures should also be suggested. Teachers must never forget to inform the parents about the interests and strengths of the child.

Although maladjustment and failures in school are lamentable, they should not blind us to the commendable success with which schools generally are able to guide the social growth and academic achievements of a majority of children. The desired role of education should not be to spotlight individual weaknesses but to provide opportunity and stimulation for every child. French novelist Anatole France had said: 'The whole art of teaching is only the art of awakening the natural curiosity of young minds for the purpose of satisfying it afterwards.' Let this be the engraved motto of each school, the solemn oath of each teacher and the sole objective of our education system.

A BAD TEACHER CAN SABOTAGE A CHILD'S CAREER

The purpose of writing this chapter is not to malign teachers, but to make parents aware of a wholly unwarranted situation. The presumption that the child is entirely responsible for his poor grades is not always true. There are some teachers, who, for a variety of reasons, may contribute—knowingly or unknowingly—towards the bad academic performance of a child.

Teachers who uniformly thwart their pupils' needs or who set goals that are unattainable by the majority of children are generally disliked. Probably the most avidly disliked teachers are the ones who not only set goals which the children cannot attain, but who also force the children to achieve them by threats and punishment.

A disliked teacher shows the following traits:

- Scolds pupils a lot
- Usually cross and bossy
- Always tries to find faults
- Has no word of encouragement
- Easily irritated and gets angry a lot
- Prejudiced and unfair

- Doesn't see things as pupils do
- Doesn't give freedom of expression and scope for improvisation
- Punitive beyond reason and not helpful
- Gives too much homework

Attitudes, prejudices, conflicts and personal-social values of teachers are unavoidably translated into behaviour patterns of children. Although a teacher is the primary source of approval or disapproval, there exists a dynamic teacher-pupil interaction within the confines of the classroom. The teacher may label the pupils as bright, dumb, compliant, wild, eager and disinterested. Similarly pupils also label their teachers as kind, vicious, attractive, unattractive, interesting, boring, reasonable and unreasonable.

A teacher's approval spurs the child to put in greater effort, while disapproval has the reverse effect. The 'approved' child brings in better results, while disapproval leads to pessimism, loss of confidence, lesser effort and persistent failure. An important role of the teacher, especially in the primary classes, is to promote the development of a positive self-concept in children. This is possible only if the teacher distributes approval and disapproval in a consistent and equitable manner. Unfortunately, a select group of children receive most of the teacher's approval. A majority of children face indifference, while a small, isolated group carries the entire burden of the teacher's disapproval. This discrimination—knowingly or unknowingly—opens the door for success for a select few, but shuts it tightly in the face of others.

As might be expected, the pupils who receive maximum teacher support and stimulation are the most intelligent ones and are already high on academic achievement. Children who are rejected, spurned or victimized by teachers have significantly lower grades and are in dire need of help. This vicious cycle goes on and on until the disapproved children fall by the wayside and are lost in the ever-increasing crowd of dropouts, delinquents and failures. This situation demands immediate attention if we wish to provide equal opportunity to all our children. Proper orientation of such teachers is urgently called for, because not only are they doing nothing to improve an already intolerable situation for frustrated and maladjusted children, but are actively damaging their future.

Rampant favouritism on the part of teachers becomes a major stumbling block for unfavoured children. Why do some teachers behave in this manner? The causes are many and the reasons varied. A favoured child may be:

- Taking private tuition from the teacher.
- From a very well-connected family.
- A ward of some faculty member.

Some teachers are themselves socially maladjusted and punitive by nature. They release their pent-up anger and aggressive tendencies by abusing the most defenceless children in their classrooms. Because of their own inadequacies and lack of confidence, they become unnecessarily and excessively annoyed by children who seem to threaten their role as disciplinarians and leaders in the classroom. Children suffer intense frustration and pain, as these teachers vent their aggressive tendencies through sarcasm, threats and physical punishment. There seems to be little excuse and absolutely no worthwhile explanation for forcing children to suffer this disgusting antipathy of a bitter teacher.

Aayushi, a Class 5 student, was brought to us by her parents, with the complaint of intractable tremors in her right hand. The tremors started suddenly, there was no other complaint and the child was generally healthy. Even on careful examination, nothing wrong was found. So, a prescription of a mild sedative and multivitamins was given, and it did the trick. However, after three months, the child was back again with even more violent tremors. This time the 'tranquilizers' failed to fully control them, as they appeared and disappeared erratically. Various investigations—including a CT scan—showed no abnormality. A detailed history revealed that Aayushi's tremors had a direct association with her examinations—they always preceded them. On gentle probing, she came out with a terrible tale of severe canning on her hands, by her teacher, for performing badly in the examinations. Counselling of the child, along with a change of 'section', made her tremors disappear permanently.

Most teachers are not unfair, prejudiced or malevolent; they simply get exasperated and frustrated by non-conforming, withdrawn and apathetic children. The patience of a teacher is put to the litmus test while dealing with children who are slow learners. The problem is compounded in the present day classrooms where sixty or more children clamour for the attention of a poor soul.

Tips for parents

Remember: The child is not always at fault! Parents must attend parent-teacher meetings and try to find out the relationship between the teacher and their ward. If the following points are observed, they must try to talk to the teacher/principal:

- If your child's academic performance deteriorates suddenly, and remains unsatisfactory.
- If a previously well-adjusted child suddenly starts showing reluctance to go to school.
- If the school diary has only adverse remarks.
- If the classwork is incomplete or wrongly done.
- If too much homework is given to the child.

26

THE UNDERACHIEVER

Aptitude tests are slowly but surely gaining currency in our country. We are convinced that they are useful, especially if done by people with the right intent and credentials. Few years back, a couple came to us with the complaint that their child is quite sharp, but his grades are very low. We asked them to get their child's aptitude test done. An aptitude test, by definition, is a type of assessment that evaluates a person's talent/ability/potential in a particular field. On the basis of the test report, we advised them to change their child's stream from Mathematics to Biology. Today, the child is studying for his MBBS degree from a prestigious institute.

We have several standard tests of intelligence, which estimate the Intelligence Quotient (IQ) of a child. The term 'underachiever' is used to indicate the child whose academic performance falls below the level of his assessed IQ.

Why should this happen? Obviously, the child is being forced to do something for which he hasn't got the aptitude. However, this is not the only cause for underachievement. Children from lower socio-economic stratas and large families are generally underachievers, too. Yet another reason is if the parents are not well-educated, especially if the mother is a school dropout. This predisposes the child towards underachievement, because enough encouragement and stimulation for academic excellence is missing.

Achievement in school is closely related to the 'level of aspiration', i.e., how well a child wishes to perform in the future, compared to how well he has done in the past. The level of aspiration is closely related to self-image and is directly proportional to the motivation and confidence level of the child. Success acts as a catalyst in this process; it increases the level of aspiration by increasing confidence and optimism. Persistent failure results in resignation, pessimism and lowering of the level of aspiration.

With the development of their conscience, children gradually become achievement-oriented. Their controls and motivation come from within, and they start feeling an urge to excel and make their parents proud and teachers happy. For this condition to develop, it is necessary for children to look up to their parents and teachers as socially, intellectually and economically superior, as persons who are dependable, and as those who love them and value their success. Unless a child has this inner drive to perform well, no amount of cajoling, compelling, enticement or punishment really works. A child who does not value success in school, generally becomes an underachiever.

Success at school is affected by, and is closely related to, the socio-economic and educational status of parents. The aim of the parents should be to provide proper perspective, motivation and emotional support. Once children imbibe the right values, they start striving harder to achieve their goals. Such support and perspective is usually lacking in children from lower socio-economic stratas, since their parents are at the bottom of the social hierarchy.

Measures to help underachievers:

- Specialized test arrangements with an easy beginning, informal and relaxed settings, and memory supports are suggested as means to help underachievers.
- Parents must provide motivation and emotional support to these children and should work in close cooperation with the school.
- When the child is on the verge of choosing his stream, generally after passing Class 10, he should preferably be asked to undergo an aptitude test. Career counselling, based on the inputs of the aptitude test, will surely benefit the child.

27

TACKLING HOMEWORK SUCCESSFULLY

It's a bitterly cold December night and the time is 9 p.m. A bitter Mrs Vaidya and her fatigued, 10-year-old daughter Saanvi, are struggling to finish the never-ending homework. They have been at it all evening, haven't had dinner and the Maths assignment is still untouched. To top it all, there is also some craft-work to be completed and handed over in the morning.

Every night, in millions of homes across the country, similar scenes are enacted with alarming regularity. The actors may be different, but the script usually remains the same. Although the problem of homework is an age-old one, the pressure of the present educational system has turned it into a recurring nightmare for most families. Homework has degenerated into a form of forced labour, in which pages upon pages of work is heaped upon the child without any scope for improvization, ingenuity or originality.

There are innumerable children like Saanvi who don't perform well in the exams even after such a back-breaking workload. Think about the parents who work throughout the day and on coming back home, sit for hours with their children, helping them with their homework. It's not difficult to visualize the frustrations of highly qualified parents, who, for example, teach nuclear physics and genetics during the day, and revert to teaching 'A cow has four legs' in the evening.

It must be said, to the credit of most parents, that they are always prepared to assist and work alongside their children on homework. The approach and methodology may vary. Some parents restrict themselves to brief occasional explanations, while others may go the extent of completing the task themselves. Children are primarily responsible for this difference in parental approach. Some children, by nature, are sincere and hardworking and are able to cope without much supervision or help. In contrast, many children have academics at the very end of their agenda, if at all. They are immune to parental cajoling or reasoning, and often, threats and bribery also fail to convince them to study. While trying to make these children do their homework, parents should take care not to get irritated, angry or disappointed.

Ten tips to tackle homework successfully:

1. Fix a Schedule

Loads of homework is given to children on a daily basis. If there is no fixed schedule for doing it, it will either remain incomplete or will be done haphazardly at the last moment, creating a lot of tension and anxiety for both, the child and the parent. As far as fixing the time is concerned, give children the liberty to decide it. Some children prefer to do their homework as soon as they return from school; others may choose to do it later in the evening. However, once the time is fixed, it should be adhered to as realistically as possible. Parents must ensure that during this period, there are no interruptions in the form of phone calls, TV, etc. Initially, parents may have to remind the child to sit down for studies, but gradually this will become a habit. Once this happens, the daily pleadings, chidings and threats may not be required and this may even improve the parent-child relationship.

2. Don't Begin with the Toughest Assignment

If children have four things to do, let them finish the three easy ones first. This makes them feel happy and relaxed because they now have only one assignment left, even though it may be a more difficult task. It also boosts their confidence and they are able to tackle the tough assignment with greater assurance. On the contrary, if the child starts with a difficult task, she may either get bogged down or spend the entire time in finishing a single assignment. This may give rise to frustration and feelings of inadequacy.

3. An Alternate Strategy

Most teachers and parents recommend reading the chapter, prior to solving questions. We think it's a good idea to read the questions before reading the chapter. By using this strategy, the child will have an idea of what he should be looking for and concentrating on, while going through the chapter. Give the child a pencil and suggest that he mark the passages that seem related to the questions given at the end of the chapter. Thus, the child will be able to pinpoint relevant, important information in the first reading itself. This will help the child when he has to refer back to several pages in the chapter in search of answers.

4. Facilitate Independent Working

Parents should try to avoid sitting next to the child while she is doing her homework. This is easier said than done, because most children stop working the moment parents stop giving them undivided attention. It's not that they can't work; they *choose* not to work. Once the child develops this dependency, she is unable to function independently in the classroom also, and will start bringing home unfinished classwork. After a busy, tiring day, when parents are faced with the prospect of sitting with the child for hours doing homework, they are likely to get frustrated and lose temper. If you are trapped in a situation where the child refuses to work without your presence and assistance, you should not break away all at once. Try to gradually get the child used to studying alone and in your absence. Initially, sit at the far end of the room for a few days. Then start moving out of the room for brief periods and gradually increase the period of your absences until the child is working alone completely. There is no fixed age when parents should give their children the responsibility of their own study. It is generally through a trial-and-error method that parents come to know whether the child is ready to take charge independently. This, however, does not mean that parents shouldn't keep track of the child's study schedule. In fact, suggestions, supervision and support will always be needed by the child at every stage of his academic life.

5. Don't Zero in on Mistakes First

While checking the child's homework, first praise him for the sums solved correctly, or for getting the spellings of difficult words right. Even for the incorrect ones, don't use criticism; instead, say, 'Please check these again. I am sure you will get the correct answers'. The child will not feel offended and will redo the problems with confidence. Some parents have a habit of zeroing in on the incorrect work first. This makes them angry and the resulting outburst greatly upsets the child. She may develop feelings of animosity or helplessness and her work, instead of improving, may actually deteriorate.

6. Split the Assignment

Most children benefit if the assignment is divided into smaller parts and immediate feedback is given. Let your child solve three problems and then come back to you for checking. Give encouragement for the correct ones and send the child back to do the next lot. By providing the child with immediate feedback and approval, you motivate him to tackle the next task with renewed vigour. Another advantage is that if the child is doing the assignment incorrectly, the error can be detected and explained right at the beginning, saving the child from having to repeat the entire assignment again. Once the child's homework is checked and ready, she will have a feeling of accomplishment and a sense of security that the work is correct. This makes the child more confident in the class and her academic performance may improve substantially.

7. Dual Input Is Better

Children retain information better if it is provided through multiple sensory inputs. It has been observed that a combination of auditory and visual inputs is more effective than either alone. Parents can audio-record some especially bothersome chapters so that the child can listen and read simultaneously. They can also record a favourite song or joke in between to cheer up the child.

8. Avoid Theatrics

Grimaces, sighs, raising of eyebrows, throwing up of hands—some parents behave as if they are enacting a tragic scene rather than helping the child with their homework. Negative body language must be avoided because it only adds to the tension of doing homework. If parents allow themselves to become agitated, they will make the child anxious and undermine her ability to perform satisfactorily.

9. Avoid Doing Your Child's Homework

Some parents don't have the time or patience to sit for hours while the child does the homework. Others may feel that the assignment is too difficult for the child to handle. Whatever the reason, when parents do their child's homework, the end result is always very damaging. The child develops a feeling of inadequacy and failure, and may become increasingly dependent upon the parents for academic work.

10. It's Better to End the Agony

If the child has been working on her assignment for quite some time without making any worthwhile progress, it's better to end her agony by stopping the homework. What the child has not accomplished in thirty minutes, is not likely to be achieved in the next three hours and thirty minutes either. Making the child sit indefinitely will only strengthen her feelings of incompetence and inadequacy. If the child is unable to do her homework once in a while, you shouldn't get worried. However, if this is a pattern, you should start looking for the cause and take remedial measures.

FIVE

EXPERTS' TIPS TO BRING UP YOUR CHILD BETTER

CHILDPROOFING YOUR HOME

A heartbreaking tragedy with one of our patients prompted us to include this topic. Let's call them the Kumars.

After a wait of ten long years, finally Mrs Kumar was pregnant. She delivered twins—two bonny boys. The firstborn was a bit underweight, but he soon caught up with his heavier sibling. The Kumars had their hands full—feeding issues, vaccinations and other minor ailments made them frequent visitors to the clinic. Although overburdened, Mrs Kumar was uncomplaining and more than willing to adhere to the advice given by us. Soon, the twins celebrated their first birthday.

However, a few days later, tragedy struck. One afternoon, when Mrs Kumar was busy with some household chore, the elder of the twins went inside the bathroom. A bucket filled with water was kept in one corner. He leaned over the brim, toppled and drowned. By the time Mrs Kumar came searching, it was a bit too late.

Most children learn to walk by 12 months of age. Once this milestone is achieved, there is no stopping them from exploring the home and its surroundings. The little ones are extremely curious about everything and anything. They will poke their fingers in the electric sockets, put all objects in their mouths and pull down things from table tops. This is the beginning of a child's active, exploring and discovering phase. To prevent accidents, the child should be provided with a safe play area. Try to childproof your home so that you can minimize the chances of injury to your child.

Useful tips for childproofing:

- Seal electric points which are placed at a low spot.
- Keep glass beads, coins and pills out of the reach of children.
- Plastic bags lying around the house are a known hazard and can cause suffocation if the child pulls the bag over his head.
- Keep children away while drinking hot beverages; most childhood burns occur due to the spilling of hot tea or coffee.
- Containers of insecticides and floor cleaners must be kept in safe custody. Mark them with a red 'X', for easy identification.
- Remove sharp-edged furniture.
- Place a soft mattress on the floor.
- Water tank must be covered to prevent drowning.
- Always keep the main door locked and hang a chime from it. If your little Einstein somehow manages to open the door, the chime will keep you informed. We are sure you don't want a rerun of *Baby's Day Out*, with your child as the protagonist.
- Keep the first-aid kit and doctor's telephone number ready.

You can make your house safe, but don't become complacent and never underestimate your kid's capabilities of landing into trouble—literally. At the same time, provide your child with many opportunities to learn and grow. Make it fun too! After all, curiosity is the mother of all learning.

29

THE THREE CRUCIAL NEEDS

Love, security and approval are the three crucial needs of every child. A child who doesn't receive love, feel secure, or get approval from the parents and other significant people around her, usually fails to attain her potential. The personality development of such children is severely compromised, and instead of adding value, they become a burden to the society.

Love and belonging

A baby is born with a need to be loved and never outgrows it. 'To love and to be loved' is the essence of all human life. A sense of belonging is crucial to a healthy personality development and successful adjustments in life. Love and warmth, imparted by the parents to their child, remain the most important determinants for developing an assured outlook towards life. Such children are also more adept at tackling problems and finding solutions. It has been rightly said: 'One who is loved can't be poor'. A child who feels loved can neither lack in confidence, nor in performance.

The feelings of love and belonging can make a child overcome several adverse circumstances, such as a physical handicap, poverty, etc. Even harsh discipline cannot dampen the spirits of a child, if they feel genuinely loved. Feelings of affection and acceptance act as cushions against disappointment, and as shields against antagonism. The best available balm for 'hurt feelings' and 'bruised egos' is the warmth exuding from the parents.

The need for close ties remains throughout life, but becomes especially important in times of stress or crisis, e.g. during examinations or at the time of a stage performance. Failing an interview is a crisis, which can be overcome easily, if the parents are forthcoming with their love and support.

Security

The need for security remains with us all our lives. Children are more vulnerable in terms of developing insecurity, because they are not yet familiar with the depravity of the world. Not knowing how to deal with a problem can upset a child. Repeated exposures to unknown and apparently threatening situations may end in acute anxiety. Feelings of insecurity can arise from interactions within the home or outside.

Sonali, 4, was brought to the clinic for a typhoid shot. On seeing her dread, I promised her a chocolate and an eraser, if she didn't cry. I was amazed by her response: 'I will not cry, otherwise the ghost will kill me. Please give the chocolate and eraser to the ghost, so he doesn't come after me.'

Sonali's father, a Sales Officer, was mostly out of town. Her mother worked in a private company and was out of the house for long hours. In their absence, Sonali's elder brother and sister were terrorizing her with imaginary ghosts living in the vicinity of their home. The missing parental care and assurance was responsible for Sonali's plight.

Lack of parental interaction and stimulation invariably leads to development of feelings of insecurity in the child.

Insecurity can also arise if the child has to cope with a domineering and demoralizing peer group. Pervasive and chronic feelings of insecurity typically lead to fearfulness, apprehension and failure to participate fully in one's world.

Approval

The approval of accomplishments is a need which must be fulfilled for further achievement. Appreciation for building a tower of three cubes encourages the child to add the fourth and the fifth cube. Praise for good manners, neat writing, or keeping the room clean, acts as a positive reinforcement and leads to the establishment of desired behaviour and self-esteem.

Self-esteem has its early foundation in parental affirmation of worth and in the mastery of early developmental tasks. When your child learns to draw a circle, don't dismiss it as being trivial. Your approval and guidance can make the child convert that circle into a human face, by adding eyes, and a nose and mouth to it. As the child develops new competencies and receives encouragement for them, his or her self-esteem gets a boost.

A child requires both approval of the parents as well as of the society. This fulfils the need to feel good about oneself and worthy of the respect of others. Achievements in areas deemed important—academics, sports, dramatics, music, etc.—help the child become more confident and develop a positive self-image.

Herbert Hoover, thirty-first President of the United States, once said, 'Children are our most natural resource'. Let us follow his advice and try to turn this vast resource into an infinite treasure.

30

TEACHING DISCIPLINE REQUIRES A LOT OF RESTRAINT

When you try to discipline your child, you are dealing with an extremely versatile and sensitive brain, capable of reasoning and decision-making. So the onus is on you to be equally reasonable, imaginative and compassionate. Regarding discipline, most parents are confused as to what constitutes too strict or too lenient an attitude. Too strict an approach is likely to cause confrontation with its built-in unpopularity. Too lenient a discipline is commensurate with disobedience, disregard and even delinquency. The three cardinal rules for effective disciplining are:

- Be realistic
- Be consistent
- Be supportive

Have guidelines and implement them consistently

Having a set of guidelines for proper behaviour is the first step in the direction of stopping impropriety. If children are bound by well-defined limits, the chances are that they will remain within them. Laxity in implementing the set rules is likely to result in unnecessary tension and frequent inappropriate behaviour. It is important that appropriate behaviour is rewarded and negative behaviour punished, but more important is the consistency of such rewards and punishments. Consistency of discipline helps the child in developing a frame of reference, which leads to a fair degree of uniformity in his behaviour pattern.

Reward and punishment

1. Reward

Who doesn't want recognition for a good work or deed? Children especially need a pat on the back for conforming to the prescribed norms of behaviour. Punishment only acts as a deterrent; it tells the child what not to do. However, rewards teach the accepted and expected behaviour. They also reinforce such behaviour and are a must if long-term changes in behaviour are desired.

Parents may feel that there is no need to reward a child for doing what is expected. But they must realize that children have only a vague concept of what is expected and what isn't. In doing what is expected, the child is making a special effort and this must be appreciated. Rewarding your child for brushing at night without being told to do so, reinforces the continuation of the habit. Rewards can be in any of the following forms:

- Monetary
- Verbal praise
- Written notes of thanks
- Extra time to play or watch TV
- A small gift
- Delayed bed time
- A spontaneous hug

2. Punishment

Choosing the appropriate punishment for inappropriate behaviour is definitely more difficult than giving rewards. Parents should avoid harsh and impractical punishments, e.g. 'no picnics or eating out till you improve your ranks'. This may dishearten the child and can cause rebellion. Even worse, you will have to sit at home on weekends, do the cooking and feed your 'convict'.

Asking the child to stand in a corner for ten minutes might be feasible, but making him stand for a full sixty minutes may be difficult to implement. Some urgent work may require your immediate attention and the child may simply vanish from the scene. Leaving a punishment incomplete will not have the desired effect; on the contrary, it can make the child more obstinate and difficult to manage.

Never trade a punishment for a reward on the 'Disciplinary Stock Exchange'. Punishment for a misdeed should not be nullified by a reward for good behaviour; both must be dealt with separately. What do you do if your child completes his homework but leaves the study table in a mess? Praise the child for finishing his assignment, but at the same time reprimand him for not cleaning the table. It would be wrong to say: 'Okay, as you have done your homework, it more than makes up for leaving your table in a mess.' If you begin trading in discipline, your child is bound to learn the trade quickly. He will prove to be an astute businessman, picking up bargain deals, but becoming undisciplined in life.

Parents must present a united front

While disciplining a child, parents must put up a united front. If one parent disagrees with the other's tactics, it should be discussed during a private moment. Open disagreement regarding a disciplinary action not only confuses the child but makes him bitter towards the seemingly unjust parent. As described earlier, if you have clear guidelines for acceptable/ unacceptable behaviour, decided mutually by both the parents, this situation need not arise.

Never ever shift the responsibility of disciplining on your spouse

'Wait until your father comes home' is a common refrain of many mothers. This must be avoided at all costs, as it gives a negative message to the child. It implies that you are incapable of controlling the situation, and this can make the child more belligerent. By relinquishing disciplinary powers to your husband, you place him in an unenviable situation. His personality acquires demonic proportions and he is forced to shout whenever he meets the children.

Disciplining is a physically and mentally draining job. Even before you finish patting yourself for successfully managing a tricky situation, a fresh crisis arises. You can run out of ideas and techniques to deal with the indiscipline of your children and your frustration levels may rise. In these circumstances, avoid dealing with children immediately. Send them to their room and tell them that you will deal with this later. Delaying allows you to regain your control and recoup your energy. A delay also reduces impractical consequences as it allows for a different perspective than that during the height of anger.

Sometimes one parent chooses to hide the child's indiscipline from another parent. This may be justified when it is done to protect the child from a parent who is known to be violent and abusive. Such protection can salvage the child's personality from total devastation. However, concealing children's inappropriate behaviour actually increases their anxiety level and they get the message that the other parent should be feared. They start fantasizing about the dire consequence should the feared parent find out their inappropriate behaviour. In most cases, it is better for the child to face the music from both speakers—one producing bass (father) and the other treble (mother).

Taming the tempest

If a child is upset or angry and speaks out his mind without being abusive or destructive, let him do so. Vocalization of frustration and anger reduces the child's tension and must be tolerated by parents. However, screaming and cursing should not be permitted, especially if it is directed at the parents. Limits must be set and the child should be taught appropriate ways of venting his feelings. Allowing the child to get away with verbal abuse can be very damaging in the long run.

Temper tantrums

Tackling temper tantrums requires a lot of patience, some firmness and a little bit of foresight. Children have a knack of choosing the most inopportune place and time for throwing a tantrum, such as a relative's place, a mall, an ice cream parlour, a toy shop, and so on. If the scene is being enacted at home, be patient and let the child calm down. However, if it occurs at a relative's or a friend's place, or any other of the above mentioned places, you have to be firm and in control. Finally, you must avoid frequent visits to toy shops and ice cream parlours when you go to the market with your child.

'Don'ts' to Deal with Temper Tantrums:

- Don't allow the child to have an audience for displaying his histrionics. Remove him to a room or any other isolated area.
- Don't try to reason with your child when he is in this state.
- Don't hesitate to tell the child that there will be a consequence later for his bad behaviour.
- Don't delay rewarding a child who checks or aborts a tantrum spontaneously to communicate with you.

For many parents, the use of discipline and reward remains a perplexing problem. But lack of consistency in dealing with inappropriate behaviour further complicates matters. Having a set of guidelines and implementing them with consistency can prevent the situation from getting out of hand. The below mentioned discipline chart is an important tool, with positive and negative consequences, which can simplify the difficult but rewarding job of raising a child:

Weekly discipline chart

Name: Grand Total: Grading:

S. No.	Rule	MON	TUE	WED	THU	FRI	SAT
1	Getting up on time						
2	Brushing teeth in the morning						
3	Punctuality at school						
4	Completing the assignments						
5	Keeping the room clean						
6	Taking proper diet						
7	Reading newspaper (headlines, at least)						
8	Not using the mobile phone unnecessarily						
9	Watching TV as permitted						

10	Helping in household chores						
11	Not cursing						
12	Participating in outdoor activity/ games						
13	Avoiding chocolates at night						
14	Brushing teeth at night						
15	Going to bed at the agreed hour						
	TOTAL						

Some Points to Remember:

- You can substitute the items as per your specific needs.
- Give 1 for compliance and 0 for non-compliance.
- Maximum achievable score is 90.
- Reward (Ice cream, Chocolate, New dress, New shoes, Visit to movies)/consequence (No TV, No eating out, Visit to mall and gaming zone cancelled) should be distributed as per the grade attained.
- Grading:
    Above 75: Good
    Between 50–75: Fair
    Below 50: Poor

31

TEN TIPS TO COMMUNICATE BETTER WITH YOUR CHILD

The ability to communicate effectively has made humans the most successful race on earth. Communication with children has two distinct aspects to it: quantity and quality. Both are important for the development of a balanced personality. Both, lack of communication and faulty communication can adversely affect the child's psyche.

Lack of communication

Children grow up so fast that parents who lose the opportunity of communicating with them when they were young, may never find meaningful and warm relationships with them in later life. Lack of communication between parents and children is the bane of modern society. The more successful the parents, the more preoccupied they are with their careers and social engagements. Naturally, in spite of their sincere efforts, they are unable to find sufficient time for their children.

TV is also an important factor that contributes to decreasing communication within the family. Most middle-class families spend their entire evenings watching never-ending serials, while children remain glued to the screen waiting eagerly for the so called 'short breaks' when the advertisements are aired. The communication-deprived children suffer from delayed speech development and show poor social adjustment capabilities. Their academic performance is also below par. The more you talk to and interact with your child, the faster her brain matures. Children who have prolonged and frequent contact with their parents not only show a higher IQ, but are also more emotionally stable and socially successful.

Faulty communication

This is perhaps even more damaging to the child's psychosocial development than mere lack of communication. Parents can alienate their children by their thoughtless uttering, thereby closing all channels for future communication. Unfortunately many parents don't realize the importance of proper communication with their children. Their communication sessions with children generally end up as sermons or arguments. The worst offenders are parents whose interaction with their children are inadequate as well as inappropriate.

Good communication skills are the basis of any successful relationship, whether between husband and wife or parents and children. Many parents face problems while communicating with their children. Knowledge of certain techniques can greatly improve their communication skills. We hope the following tips will help parents to communicate better with their children:

Communication = Talking + Listening

The most common mistake that parents make is that they talk, but never listen. While communicating, the flow of ideas and thoughts should necessarily be bidirectional, otherwise it becomes a lecture. The child must know that when you finish talking, he will get a chance to speak. Try listening actively. Make encouraging gestures and sounds—nod your head and say 'yes', 'all right' and 'that's fine'.

Avoid: 'You listen to me.'

Try: 'I want you to listen to me first, and then you can speak and I'll listen.'

Don't Begin with an Accusation

If you start the conversation with an accusation, the child will end it with a brief refusal. If your opening line is: 'Why did you break the wall clock?', the most likely answer you'll get is: 'I didn't'.

A better way to approach the situation would be to ask: 'How did the clock break?' This will get the conversation going, and you will receive a detailed account of the events leading to the breaking of the clock. You can also utilize this opportunity to teach the child to be more responsible in the future.

Avoid: 'I don't believe you.'

Try: 'Promise not to lie and I'll believe you.'

Avoid Flowery Language

Reserve your eloquence for boardroom meetings, farewell parties and the like. While communicating with children, it is better to keep things straight and simple. This is especially important when dealing with a relatively young child because more often than not, the child will either miss the point or misinterpret it. In case of older children, use of flowery language can injure their pride and give them an inferiority complex.

Avoid: 'You are an idiot of the highest order.'
Try: 'You need to apply yourself more.'

Avoid: 'Your room is worse than a pigsty.'
Try: 'Your room needs urgent cleaning.'

Words Are Like Bullets

There is no denying the power of spoken words; they are more potent than bullets. You can use them to attack or protect your child's personality. If children feel they are being attacked, they may:

- Clam up
- Start arguing
- Throw counter-accusations

All the three situations interrupt the flow of communication and may alienate the child. As a rule, communication will deteriorate if you use intimidating language. Parents who try to browbeat their child all the time, may succeed initially, but gradually the child will start paying back in the same currency. While dealing with children, mild attitude and milder vocabulary usually produces the desired result.

Avoid: 'Come here immediately.'
Try: 'Let's get together in five minutes.'

Avoid: 'I want you home by 6 p.m., positively.'
Try: 'Please be home between 6 and 6.30 p.m.'

Prevent Misinterpretation

Remember, children are not expert face readers, so they cannot decipher the real reason behind your grim expression. In most instances they will misread the look on a parent's face and presume that they have done something wrong. If parents are upset or angry because of a job-related problem, or there is some other reason, they must verbally let their children know about it. There is no need to go into details; just tell the child: 'Something/someone has made me very angry, but it has nothing to do with you. Let me have tea and rest for a while, then I'll feel much better.' This small, thoughtful piece of communication can not only relieve the child's anxiety, but also make him more favourable towards you.

Written Notes Are Great

There are occasions when you need to communicate your feelings in writing. Parents and children should use this method more often as written communication gives an opportunity to phrase thoughts more coherently. Notes praising children for good behaviour, helping in housework or doing well in studies are great morale boosters. Parents can pleasantly surprise their children by slipping a message in their pencil box or notebook, saying that they love them very much, or that they are proud of them. Notes can also be used to register a complaint, without creating a scene. When you expect a showdown or want to avoid an unnecessary argument, written notes are the best way to show your displeasure.

Wordless Communication

An important means of communicating with children is through eye contact and change of facial expression. When you are socializing or in a setting where it is not possible to give verbal commands, you can show your approval or disapproval by an encouraging or a stern look, respectively. Success of this form of communication depends upon prior conditioning of the child. In spite of your best training, sometimes the child may avoid your eyes to act according to his wishes. Don't get upset; children after all, are children.

Demonstrative Communication

All human beings are born with a need to be loved and never outgrow this need. When it comes to communicating feelings of love and care, many parents are found wanting. Many of us got our first real proof of parental love when we fell sick. This indirectly indicates that illness, injury and other adverse situations are a prerequisite for receiving love and care. That should not be the case. Parents must take care that children do not get such a distorted picture of the parent-child relationship. The line, 'If you love somebody, show it', may sound clichéd, but it nevertheless holds true for many parents. Try to demonstrate your love, show you care and express your feelings.

Demonstrative communication can be 'verbal' or 'physical'. Some verbal statements you can use are:

- 'I am really proud to have a son/daughter like you.'
- 'If I scold you, it doesn't mean that I don't love you.'
- 'I am lucky to have such a conscientious/dependable/ meticulous child like you.'

Don't *assume* your child knows that you feel this way; communicate to him in your own words.

Physical demonstration of feelings is also very important for the development of a warm and loving parent-child relationship. Never miss an opportunity to hug, kiss or cuddle your child. If you don't give love today, your child will not learn to receive it tomorrow—neither from you nor from anyone else. It has been observed that such children are non-demonstrative themselves and may have unproductive relationships in later life. Children who had plenty of emotional and physical contact with their parents find it easier to give and receive love.

Supportive Communication

For the proper expression of emotions and to sustain communication, a good vocabulary is a must. Children may face problems while communicating because they lack experience in labelling their feelings. When children fail to find appropriate words and are unable to correctly verbalize their internal feelings, they are likely to become frustrated. Frustration may cause behavioural problems and destructive tendencies. Sometimes in their haste, they may choose wrong words and offend their parents. Thus, the process of communication may deteriorate into an argument.

Parents must therefore help their children to correctly label a feeling or emotion. Here are some examples that can be used to assist the child:

- 'I get the feeling from your behaviour that you are trying to say you have been wrongly blamed for the broken glass.'
- 'While you sound angry, it is actually your frustration over not being able to finish the project given to you by your teacher.'
- 'I guess you want to communicate that you want to go for a sleepover at your friend's home.'

Anticipatory Communication

A good parent can anticipate the child's mood and reaction to a situation. If you are observant enough, you can see some non-verbal reaction: a dull look, a deadpan face, brimming eyes or intense denial. If you can comprehend these expressions, you will have instant knowledge of the child's emotional turmoil. The child will also have an easier time communicating to you because he can sense your involvement and concern. Parents who are good at anticipatory communication have a very good chance of identifying and dealing with the child's problems.

32

SODAS

Every child and most adults love ice cream sodas. Cola-Shooter and Pina-Orange are our family's favourites. You must be wondering what ice cream sodas have to do with parenting. Don't be surprised; we aren't discussing ice cream sodas here.

SODAS stands for:

S = Situation

O = Options

D = Disadvantages

A = Advantages

S = Solution

It is an acronym for a simple problem-solving method that is easy for young children and the youth to learn, understand and use. It was developed by counsellor Jan Rosa in 1973. It can be effectively taught by role playing situations faced by the characters of television programmes that are popular with kids. It could also be practised through written exercise. This method is often best understood when a child or teen uses it immediately after being involved in a situation in which he got into trouble or faced an outcome that he was not happy with. Providing kids with small items, such as a keychain with a miniature soda bottle is a tangible way to reinforce this method.

This is how it works:

1. **S = Situation:** The child describes a situation. For example: 'Jitesh cursed me, so I punched him in the nose. The teacher sent me to the principal's office and they called you (Dad/Mom).'

2. **O = Options:** The child is encouraged to list at least three options he could have considered for handling this situation. It is important that the option (punching in the nose) that caused the problem (being sent to the principal's office) is still included as one of the possibilities. For example:

   Option 1: I could go and tell my teacher that Jitesh cursed me.

   Option 2: I could ignore it, and go and find someone else to play with.

   Option 3: I could punch Jitesh when he curses me.

(Note: It's okay if the child can think of more than three options for any particular situation.)

3. **D = Disadvantages** and **A = Advantages:** Next, the child lists some disadvantages and advantages (pros and cons, or benefits and consequences) for each of the options. It is important to include both disadvantages and advantages for each option. For example:
   - For Option 1:
     - Disadvantage—I get a reputation of a 'snitch' (an informant/sycophant of teachers) at school.
     - Advantage—The teacher helps me solve the problem; I do not get into any trouble.

- For Option 2:
  - Disadvantage—I didn't express my anger, so I am still frustrated.
  - Advantage—Jitesh sees he can't get to me by cursing, so maybe he won't do it again and I won't get in trouble.
- For Option 3:
  - Disadvantage—I get sent to the principal and they call my Dad/Mom.
  - Advantage—I express my anger and maybe Jitesh would be afraid to curse me again.

4. **S = Solution:** Finally, after reviewing several options—each with its disadvantages and advantages—the child or teen comes up with a solution for 'next time'. For example: One child may decide that Option 2 will be better, while another child may be willing to be called a 'snitch' for the sake of getting help from the teacher to deal with his problem.

Follow-up and practise

Parents can help their children—both young and old—use this method as a proactive and preventive strategy, by following up and asking them (at dinner perhaps) if they had any opportunities to 'do a SODAS' today. Children often enjoy having opportunities to practise the steps using funny or unusual situations, as well as 'typical' situations that they often face. Also, it is helpful if parents demonstrate how they use this method to solve problems or make decisions of their own.

SODAS Worksheet	
1. Describe the **Situation**:	
2. List 3 or more **Options** for handling this situation next time: a. b. c. d.	
3. For *each* option, list the **Disadvantages** and **Advantages**	
DISADVANTAGES	ADVANTAGES
Option a	Option a
Option b	Option b
Option c	Option c
Option d	Option d
4. What is my **Solution**?	

This may appear time-consuming initially, but with practice, it can be done within five minutes. If your child is facing frequent behavioural or adjustment problems at school or in the neighbourhood, SODAS can prove to be a real boon for him. It will help him develop the capability to deal with day-to-day challenges with patience and equanimity—the trademark of a winner!

33

YOU TOO CAN MAKE YOUR CHILD A LEADER

All children are born with the same number of chromosomes. They also have an identical brain structure and similar body functions. The 'edge' comes from mental attitude, character and strategizing. It is in these vital areas that parents have to help their children, so that not only do they achieve their potential, but exceed it. Success and self-belief join hands to make a leader out of an ordinary person. What you have learned through your own experiences must be analysed and passed on to your children, to help them remain a step ahead of the competition. Let us share some secrets on how to develop leadership qualities in your child.

Begin early

A leadership mentality will benefit the child at all stages of her life. It has been observed that leadership qualities developed during school years and achievements in extracurricular activities are more accurate predictors of adult success than IQ or examination percentage. Nurturing self-esteem is the central element in inspiring a child to perform well, and you can't start too early because in case the feelings of incompetence or inadequacy take root, they become very difficult to remove.

What you put in is what you get back

We all know that if we provide a nutritious diet to a child, she will grow to be healthy. This applies to character development also. If parents are the epitome of good behaviour, truthfulness and punctuality, then it is easier for their children to develop these traits. It is foolhardy to expect that you can extract gold by processing iron ore. Instilling proper values will make a child grow their inner strength. The associated confidence will transform her into a leader.

Assess your child's potential

Wrong assessment of the child's potential and an attempt to mould her in a way that is contrary to her natural ability can lead to disaster. Although listening to the child's views is recommended, it is possible that her self-assessment may stem from inexperience. There is no harm in taking help from an expert in shaping your child's future.

According to a newspaper report, the modern cricketing legend, Sachin Tendulkar, had gone to Dennis Lillee, the great Australian fast bowler, to learn the art of pace bowling. Lillee was not impressed by the young boy—at all. A few years later, Lillee saw Tendulkar's batting and this time he was highly impressed with the young man's brilliant ability to score shots. Sachin's coach, Ramakant Achrekar, had turned him into an explosive, high-class batsman. Today, even after retirement, Sachin remains an inspiration for every budding Indian cricketer and is regarded as one of the best batsmen ever.

Focus on inappropriate behaviour, not personality

Unfortunately, instead of pointing out unacceptable behaviour, most parents point a finger at the child: 'You are so dumb!', 'Why can't you get it through your thick skull?', 'God, you are such a clumsy, insufferable fool.' However, you should criticize the behaviour, not the child. After saying, 'That's wrong!', explain what's right. You must let your children know what you want them to do; not just what you *don't* want them to do.

Remember, your child is not stupid! If she fails to measure up to your yardsticks of excellence, lower them or put in a concerted effort to raise the child's standard. Children who grow up in homes where personalities are attacked, tend to develop an inferiority complex.

When confronting the child's act, try using phrases like: 'Poor judgment', 'This is not how it is done' and 'Your behaviour was inappropriate'. Focusing on the act allows children to save face. It may also allow them to better understand and accept more appropriate options for the next time. When children learn to behave appropriately at home, they carry this behaviour to the outside world also. This will certainly improve their popularity—especially among their peers. Gaining acceptance in the peer group gives children opportunities to interact, influence and lead other children.

Don't be a miser with praise

Praise is the best tonic for self-esteem, and applause is the greatest booster of self-confidence. Children who are confident and have a high self-esteem are natural leaders. When your little one takes her first few unsteady steps towards you, or when she climbs up the stairs and declares triumphantly from the top, 'I am the tallest', your look of genuine pleasure and approval makes her grow in self-esteem. Even a hesitant child may accomplish the feat if she is told, 'I know you can do it!' And if the parents follow it up with, 'You did a terrific job', the child's confidence gets a boost. Many world-class sportspersons, singers, musicians and academicians readily concede that the primary influence on their early career was their parents' support and appreciation. Talking positively about children and their accomplishments reinforces self-image and goads them to strive for further excellence. It is through exemplary performance that one finally becomes a leader. However, as mentioned earlier, be judicious with your praises—do it, but don't overdo it.

Think about success, not obstacles

'What if I fail?' (The class test)
'What if I forget?' (The speech during elocution)
'What if I miss?' (The goal)

Individuals, who, instead of focusing on how to succeed, keep worrying about how to avoid failure, generally end up as disappointments. Parents should try to develop the right values and a positive attitude in their wards. They should persuade them to concentrate on success and be pragmatic about failures, treating them as temporary setbacks. The person who believes in success is the one who can inspire others to follow.

Build on previous accomplishments

If your child has won a medal in a debate competition, a cup in athletics or a certificate of merit in academics, display it prominently in the house. Whenever the child sees it, she will get an urge to do better. Confining oneself to previous triumphs is not advisable, but using them as an inspiration for additional success is recommended. By seeing the previously won medals and trophies, the child gets the message: 'I have done it in the past; I can do it again.' This 'can do' approach can make your child a leader.

Teach your child to relax

The ability to remain calm during a crisis makes one the ace of the pack—the leader. Teach your child to relax, because anxiety leads to poor concentration, which is the root cause of poor performance. A relaxed mind can think and act better, thus improving the efficiency of a person.

An extremely effective technique to relax is to breathe deeply and evenly. Train the child to concentrate on each inhalation and exhalation and to let his mind go blank for a few moments. Thinking of a favourite song, imagining a flowing river or a cool breeze blowing gently—any pleasant idea can be utilized to put the child in a relaxed mood.

Let children experiment

We admire and follow someone who is willing to experiment and rise to challenges. Yet, when it comes to our own children, we want them to play safe. All too often, we step in and try to stop a child from making mistakes. In the process, we deprive her of important learning experiences.

Parents should motivate the child to take initiative and tackle new challenges. The one who tries, fails, rectifies her mistakes and gets up to make a fresh attempt, finally succeeds. This spirit of adventure and steely resolve sets one apart as a leader. A true leader is one who rises to the occasion without fear of failure and is able to inspire others by her enthusiasm.

Leaders are dreamers

If your son wants to be a fighter pilot or your daughter wants to become a crime reporter, what would your response be? 'It's risky business! Why can't you think of something less dangerous?'

The chances are your son may want go into aero-designing and your daughter might want to become a computer programmer. Don't overreact; let children fantasize about the future. Who knows? They may devise means and find ways to make their fantasies come true.

To see things, you should have the vision; to visualize the future, you must have dreams. Leaders have this vision and they can dream. They look at things differently and can explain them to others, and are able to influence people into following their path. So, let children dream, but tell them that the best way to make their dreams come true is to wake up and work—as all leaders do.

Give children opportunities to lead

Leadership, like any other skill, has to be learnt, practised and mastered. Just as a tennis player must practise hard to perfect her serve, a would-be leader must be provided ample opportunities to imbibe leadership skills.

Motivate the child to become a member of the NCC, National Service Scheme (NSS), Scouts or other such groups, which will give them a platform to interact with and lead other children. A captain of a school football team, a class monitor or a school prefect—all are learning the craft of leadership. Parents must encourage this early apprenticeship, but the child should be allowed to pursue her own areas of interest. Alternatively, parents must allow their children to operate in their favoured domain, which builds their confidence and lays the foundation of leadership. Some children revel on stage, some shine on the playground, while others excel in the classroom—let the leader in your child come to the fore and choose her field.

A smile takes you a mile

It requires sixty-four facial muscles to frown and only fourteen to smile. So, why overwork your face? A friendly 'hello' and a pleasant smile can win many a battle. Teach your child to not only greet those in her own circle, but others as well. Instil in her, human values and respect for elders. A person who exudes natural warmth and genuine compassion, not just to relatives but also others, is quickly recognized as a potential leader.

Your example matters

It has been seen that when parents exhibit leadership qualities, it becomes easier for children to develop similar traits. Parents who set high standards of moral and ethical conduct generally succeed in teaching the same to their children—like begets like. A thief can't expect his son to be a virtuous, law-abiding citizen. Similarly, an honest, resourceful father is likely to have a respectful, responsible son.

A shortcut to success has not yet been successfully developed. The making of a leader is a gradual process that requires parental support, encouragement and hard work. These efforts are doubly rewarding: Your child develops the qualities of a leader and more importantly, you form a close and warm relationship with your child.

34

SMART PARENTS RAISE SMART KIDS

How your children grow up will depend not just on the amount of care you give them, or how much money is spent on them, but on how smartly all this is done. How informed the parents are, and their efficiency in tackling everyday situations are the key determinants of their children's success.

If you want your children to succeed in life, you have to act with responsibility, restraint, equanimity and patience. You have to be clear and firm while dealing with your children, but not at the cost of a warm, loving and mutually gratifying relationship. Raising a child is very much like building a skyscraper. If the first few storeys are out of line, no one will notice. But when the building is eighteen- or twenty-storeys high, everyone will see that it's tilted. This means you have to begin early, before the child goes on a wrong track. Bringing the child back on the right track will require much more effort than not letting him proceed on one.

Throughout this book we have laid emphasis on the use of common sense while dealing with your child. Here again, we give you inputs regarding the clever handling of day-to-day situations at home.

Conserve your energy

All of us have a certain amount of physical and mental energy to use in dealing with the everyday activities and stresses of life. Unnecessary conflicts tend to drain our energy and so, less energy is available to keep things in proper perspective. This means that you have to choose your battlegrounds wisely. Sit down with your child and discuss what you feel are the key issues. Once you have identified them, frame a set of guidelines and channelize your energy to see that they are followed. If you keep reacting to trivial issues, you will have little energy left to deal with the more important problems.

I will try to explain this by equating energy with money. Decide whether an issue is worth ₹10, ₹100, or ₹1,000, and then spend your energy in accordance with the importance of the issue. Overspending can only lead to an early burnout.

If your child spills a glass of milk, think of the following before you start hollering:

1. Was it a mistake? If yes, you don't have any right to shout; even you can make a mistake.
2. Was it deliberate? If yes, think about the cost: ₹10, which is negligible. The only issue worth dealing with is the indiscipline of the child. Talk to him and explain that doing so was inappropriate. Also warn him about the unpleasant consequence of repeating such behaviour in the future.

The importance of saying 'no'

Once we had gone out for dinner with a family we know very well. As we came out of the restaurant, their 5-year-old son Tushar saw a hawker selling toy cars. He demanded a particular car and, when refused, started whining, which soon grew to wailing and finally, shrieking with rage. His parents were almost tempted to buy him the car, but their momentary hesitation gave us the opening we were looking for. We told them to deal with the situation firmly and not to succumb to the irrational demand of their child. On the way back, Tushar's cries drowned the music from the car stereo by many a decibel. When we dropped them at their gate, his cries had changed to a whimper. We were later informed that Tushar was off to sleep the moment he was put to bed and when he got up in the morning, he had forgotten all about the car.

Giving in to a child's demands is the easiest way out—the path of least resistance. But if you do it all the time, you will spoil your child. Not only will his demands increase, they will become more and more irrational.

Children are the worst victims of the advertising blitzkrieg on television. Advertisements for new toys, dolls, chocolates, electronic games and bicycles fire their imagination and increase their cravings. They are easily sold on to new ideas and things, and when they are unable to acquire them, they become frustrated. Parents have to guide children to strike a balance between unreasonable demands and reasonable fancies. Here's what you should do:

1. *Money Matters*: Don't buy expensive gifts in a casual off-hand manner. If your child wants a new bicycle and you feel it is justified, you should say: 'Although you do need a new bicycle, still we will have to discuss it. You can't go to the market and pick up a bicycle just like that.' From the very beginning make it clear to your children that whatever you buy for them, or for yourself, involves serious decision-making. Also tell them that

many things are useless and not worth buying. They must get the message that money is not an unlimited commodity and it must be spent wisely. If you use prudence in indulgence, it will not harm your child.

2. ***Don't Feel Guilty***: Working parents feel that because they're unable to give sufficient time to their children, they should somehow compensate for their absence. They get into the habit of buying gifts to overcome their feeling of guilt. While this may make the parents feel generous, it is harmful for children as they start demanding gifts and treats all the time. Don't feel guilty! By working, you are in a position to provide a good living standard, better entertainment and the best education to your child. Instead, try to find time for your child and take interest in his interests. Avoid bringing home the files and frustrations of your office.

3. ***Stick to Your Guns***: The primary reason why parents give in to their children's irrational demands is to avoid a 'scene'. Once you say 'no', it should remain a 'no'! When you deliver a firm 'no', the child gets the message that crying and cajoling will not get him anywhere. Also, while doing so, you must try to offer the simplest explanation for your refusal. If your daughter demands a new pair of party shoes and you know she doesn't need them, don't beat about the bush by saying: 'They appear quite flimsy', 'They are not worth their price', or 'Having so many shoes is unjustified'. Such reasoning may sound okay to an adult, but it is beyond the comprehension of children. Simply tell her: 'You don't need new shoes.' If your child manages to have her own way by crying, pleading or pestering, she will quickly master the technique and make your life miserable. When the child is creating a scene inside a

shop, it is better to let it happen. Stand by your decision, even if your child's 'wailing' makes you look heartless. If necessary, catch hold of your child and leave the shop—sometimes you have to be rigid to prove a point. As parents, your job is to help your children decide what's worth getting and what isn't. You should teach them that there are better ways of raising demands and getting them fulfilled. They must learn that throwing a tantrum, screaming or crying will not achieve anything.

Remain optimistic about your child's capabilities

Parents who use praise and rewards, instead of criticism and punishment, generally obtain positive results. They are able to eliminate undesired behaviour and reinforce desired behaviour in their children. Parents must look at the brighter side of the child and highlight his competencies and accomplishments. Focusing on the weaknesses and blaming him for minor lapses can prove to be counterproductive.

Neha, 13, was brought to my clinic with the complaints of general weakness and poor memory. She was unable to retain anything and was performing poorly in her studies. Her parents had already administered to her a variety of the so called 'memory enhancing' tonics, but to no effect. While talking to her, I was pleasantly surprised by her clear and precise diction. Her parents also confirmed that she always spoke very clearly and with correct pronunciations, even when she was a little girl.

I instinctively enquired whether she had ever participated in a speech or a debate competition—the answer was in the negative. I suggested that she should enter her name whenever an opportunity came her way.

At the end of the consultation, I wrote out two prescriptions.

Neha's prescription contained an iron tonic, as she was mildly anaemic.

Her parents' prescription was:

i.   Motivate Neha to participate in a speech/debate competition.
ii. Give her full support—emotional as well as material—when she decides to participate.

Two months later, a beaming Neha entered my clinic with her parents. She was holding an impressive trophy in her hands, which she had won in an inter-school speech competition. She stood first among some fifty children from eighteen leading schools of the city. The topic was 'Eliminate Child Labour'. No doubt, her parents had helped her in writing the speech, but it was Neha who delivered it with aplomb.

The victory gave a tremendous boost to Neha's confidence and she developed faith in her abilities. This started reflecting in her improved academic performance as well, and her 'memory problem' became a thing of the past.

Give children some responsibility

You can't teach 'responsibility', but you can make a child 'responsible'. Yuvraj, 12, was an incorrigible little brat—lazy, irritable and generally disinterested. He loved to watch 'any damn thing' on television and his only contribution in the house was maintaining it in a state of perpetual mess.

Ultimately, his parents decided to involve him in running the household. Yuvraj was given the responsibility for purchasing the monthly grocery. His parents were to guide him in this endeavour. He was given a certain amount of money, equivalent to the average monthly expenditure on grocery, at the beginning of the month. He was also provided with a diary to maintain a record of the purchases. If any money was left at the end of the month, it went to his kitty.

Today, Yuvraj has no time for television—he is a busy young 'businessman'. He has learned to save and to spend wisely. His arithmetic marks and his 'bank balance' both have improved substantially.

Practise what you preach

One of the most significant ways children learn what to do and what not to do is by watching their parents. So be careful, you are their first and foremost role model—sooner or later they will imitate your actions and behaviour.

If you shout to get your way, expect your children to do the same. If you remain sprawled on a sofa watching television instead of finishing urgent household chores, your children will also learn to defer doing their homework. If you want to inculcate reading habits in your child, start reading yourself. If you want your child to say 'sorry' and 'thank you', you better start using these words yourself. When your child sees you apologizing for a mistake, he will quickly learn to do the same.

Heads: I win; Tails: you lose

Choose two options that are both acceptable to you, and then ask the child to decide which one of the two he prefers. Whatever the child's decision, it leaves you happy and smiling. For example, ask the child whether he would like to study in the night for the exam or to get up early in the morning. Either way, you ensure that your child prepares for the exam. If instead of 'either', the child replies 'neither', remind him that 'neither' is not an option and he has to choose from the two offered. Just hold your nerves; your child will make a choice within a few minutes.

If you adopt an open-ended approach and ask the child: 'When would you like to study for your exam?', you may either get no response or one that is not acceptable to you. Smart parents make it appear that it is the child who is making the choice.

Don't play Sherlock Holmes

You return home from work and switch on the TV for the latest news, but the screen remains dark. Your latest acquisition—a 42-inch LED TV, which you left in perfect working condition in the morning—has conked out. You call over your children and, pointing to the TV, thunder: 'Who did it?'

Your children will vehemently deny coming anywhere near the television. It will be almost impossible to actually find out 'who did it', as they will keep blaming each other.

Your child is a potent combination of Vasco da Gama and Archimedes. He is eager to know more and is driven by the spirit for adventure. But if your luck runs out, this might turn into a misadventure. The question, 'Who did it?', creates a situation where the child feels cornered and the fear of punishment makes him point an accusing finger at a sibling or a servant. By asking 'who', you convey that your intention is to find out and punish the guilty. Whether the child has done it or not, he will usually answer, 'Not me', and try to shift the blame on others.

If instead, you ask, 'How did it happen?', you will have a better chance of getting a response. Call your children and point out the problem. If they accuse each other, tell them you are not interested in knowing who did it, but in knowing why the television is not working. Your children are sure to feel bad about damaging the TV and are likely to be more responsible in future. Finally, it may turn out to be just a case of a blown fuse, and there was absolutely no need for you to have blown your fuse as well.

Don't be a 'Super Parent'

Adarsh was launched on the path of success from the moment his umbilical cord was cut. When he was a little baby, his father fortified him with a multitude of multivitamin syrups, while his mother tried to strengthen his body by massaging him with pure olive oil.

Now, his parents strive hard to ensure that he always ranks first, whether it is in academics, sports, dancing, painting, singing or debating. While talking to Adarsh, their favourite words are: 'vital', 'urgent', 'significant', 'important' and 'at the end of the day'. During the weekends, they ferry him to and from endless tuitions and coaching throughout the day. The evenings are again devoted to achieving academic excellence.

Yes! Adarsh's parents are 'Super Parents' and they want him to be a 'Super Kid'. They have unlimited energy and are so highly charged that they just can't relax. Their devotion towards the success of their child can give an inferiority complex to us 'ordinary' and 'normal' parents. By seeing them operate at full throttle always, we may sometimes be forced to verify our antecedents and credentials as good parents.

Super Parents are so busy running and doing things for their children, that they miss out on just being with their children. They get trapped in their own frantic drive to succeed, and fail to forge an emotional and mental bonding with their children. By their exacting standards and demands for perfection, they put extreme pressure on their children, who start feeling guilty and unworthy if they fail to live up to the super expectations of their Super Parents. Thus, unknowingly, they make their children anxious and unhappy.

Some people may argue in favour of Super Parents, but they should sit back and think a while! Who is benefitting from all these efforts? Are you making your child miserable because of your own needs for glory? Is he being sacrificed at the altar of your ego? If yes, then perhaps it's time for you to drop the facade of being a Super Parent and make a sincere effort at becoming a normal parent.

Learn to breathe easy

Children will make mistakes; they will do silly, mischievous or thoughtless things. Parents must maintain their cool and behold a sense of dignity. When parents tend to forget their own childhood, and its trials and joys, things get complicated. Take a few deep breaths and try to calm down. It's hard to think clearly when you're angry and you might forget every sensible thing you know about good parenting. However, one of the best ways to become a better parent is to batter your anger, not your child.

35

THE ROLE OF A FATHER

To some, fatherly instincts come naturally, but others have to develop them—and develop they must—because fathers have a unique presence and place in the family. Their role in cultivating mutual trust and binding the family together is undisputed. Their unconditional love or persistent apathy can be the vital difference between the success and failure of the child. Good fathers have a stimulating and playful relationship with their children. They are more likely than mothers to teach physical skills and enterprise, and can help the child to be confident and assertive in adverse situations. Children of such fathers show good social adjustment, handle peer pressure better and generally score higher on intelligence tests. A good father doesn't make promises he can't keep. He delivers even when he hasn't promised. Are you a good father? Check it out!

Don't shirk housework

A father's contribution in housework has always been, and still remains, a contentious issue. Generally, the entire responsibility of running the household lies with the mother, even though she may herself be in a full-time job. Winds of change are gathering momentum and there is a perceptible difference in the attitudes of the new generation.

In the past, fathers used to be pretty remote characters, but today, many men actively share the responsibilities of parenthood with their wives. To them, preparing the feed for the baby is as important as readying a project report. I am quite sure my father never changed a nappy, but I am quite adept at it. I must have changed hundreds of wet nappies of my two daughters. My wife has always been quite appreciative of the fact, and is of the firm belief that all women should preferably marry paediatricians.

A father who is a good cook is like a prince in shining armour. When he is in the kitchen, cooking one of his specialties, the entire family joins in to help. Can there be a stronger glue to bind the family together? Sons of such fathers are likely to master culinary skills and become 'special' fathers themselves.

You don't have to be a master chef to be a good father. You can begin by boiling eggs and later on, graduate to making omelettes, sandwiches and shakes. If you can't accomplish these tasks, don't lose heart; there are other avenues to show your mettle. You can lay the table, take things out from the fridge and heat them, fill the water bottles and ice trays—the list is endless. By seeing you help your wife in the kitchen, your children will also be motivated to learn these chores.

Some fathers have a technical bend of mind and an aptitude for fixing things. Your children will love to join you while you repair a leaking tap or a blown fuse. We would advise you to spend five minutes during weekends to oil and grease your child's bicycle. He will love it!

Moving with the times

As compared to mothers, fathers generally tend to become 'outdated' sooner. So, keep your eyes wide open and ears finely tuned for 'change'. From being a toddler, to becoming a teenager, your child makes rapid progress. You must also move with the times and keep in touch with your child's changing tastes. You should be well-informed about the recent trends in clothing, food fads and teenage 'lingo' (slang). Remember: Children are very prompt in labelling their fathers as ancient/vintage!

A conservative doctor-friend of mine was quite upset with the dress sense of his gawky, teenaged daughter. Her revealing attire and dazzling make-up would be enough to blind any parent with fury. When he looked around, he found that most girls of her age were more or less similarly dressed in skimpy, body-hugging dresses. Rather than admonishing her, my friend figured that by aping them, his daughter was simply trying to be part of her peer group. By making a clothing statement and by her flair for wisecracks, she not only became a part of the gang, but in fact, was leading it.

During the annual club dinner, our families happened to share the same table. Even though my friend's daughter was wearing her usual tight black dress and a terrifying luminescent eye shadow, her behaviour was exemplary. She chatted with us confidently and even entertained us with her funny remarks about the 'best dancing couple of the eve'.

I am sure in a few years' time she will become more responsible and prove to be a successful young lady. Her father's confidence in her and eventual acceptance of her as she was, were the two most important factors in building her confidence and self-esteem. Criticism and rejection by her father would surely have alienated her, damaged her personality and given her an inferiority complex.

Find time for your children

You may be very busy making mega-deals, conceptualizing and implementing huge projects, but don't do it at the cost of neglecting your children. When you are back at home, don't push away your children, saying, 'Leave me alone'. You can't make a worse investment for the future. Remember, time and love are the two most important things your kids need and desire from you. It is not always necessary for you to talk; your simple presence and a crisp 'yes' and 'no' to their queries is sufficient for them to feel at peace.

If you are working in the garden, call your children—not for help, but to listen to their banter and to share your day's experiences. If you are working on the computer and there are no deadlines to be met, let your child operate the mouse for a while and, later, appreciate his help. Sometimes, I sit down on the dining table to write, and ask my daughters to come and sit with me to finish their homework. They do disturb me, but it is a small price to pay for their companionship and to gain the label of a considerate father.

There are hordes of activities to get involved in. You can play indoor/outdoor games, or go cycling, trekking or fishing. All children love kite-flying—use this opportunity to form a team with your child. If both parents are working, the family should at least have dinner together. A stimulating discussion at dinnertime can make the food seem warmer than that heated by a microwave, and exciting news can make even insipid food taste like spicy Mexican cuisine.

Fathers who have to do a lot of job-related travelling, or who are in the armed forces/merchant navy and have to be away from the home for prolonged periods, should try to maintain constant contact with their children. They can call, email or WhatsApp their children to keep the relationship blossoming.

Lack of paternal supervision has been related to low IQ and poor academic performance. Children from such homes show a high incidence of violent behaviour and delinquency. They are also more prone to drug addictions. Paternal involvement is vital to an all-round personality development in a child. Close interaction with the father enhances a child's reasoning and independence, and instils leadership qualities.

Express your love

When Alisha's parents returned home from work, they noticed that their 9-year-old daughter was not her usual chirpy, bubbly self. She looked dull, dejected and spiritless, and was wandering around the house aimlessly. When her worried parents questioned her, she broke down into tears but kept on shaking her head saying, 'It's nothing'.

Finally, her father sat down with her, took her hand and tenderly questioned her until he learned the cause of her sadness. Alisha had practised hard and had memorized all her lines, but still her teacher had removed her from the play to be staged on the annual day. Gently and simply, he talked to her about life, opportunities, striving and success. He comforted her and didn't dismiss the episode as trivial, but treated her with dignity and concern.

Alisha's father was expressing his love for his daughter, giving her his time and trying to see the world through her eyes and from her perspective. What he was doing would qualify as an ideal form of fathering. No doubt, you love your child, but may find it difficult to show it. Don't lose heart; this is a common ailment among fathers. If you feel you have problems expressing affection, make special efforts: Write it in a letter or give a card which says what you always wanted to say, but couldn't because of your inhibitions. You can write an admiring note on the back of one of your child's drawings. I myself can't be called a very demonstrative father, but my skills at writing poetry has kept me 'in business'. My daughters may not think I am a great poet, but they do feel that the poems I write for them are a true expression of my love. Most children wish their fathers would tell or show them in some way, that they really love them. Many adults concede that they can't recall their fathers ever hugging or kissing them, or saying they loved them. Illnesses probably are the only occasions when fathers allow the clouds of indifference to clear and let their concern shine through.

Some children feel uncomfortable with public displays of affection, especially when friends are around. Make no mistake—they still need your love and encouragement, but in a subtle, covert manner. When your child is about to participate in a sports activity or perform on the stage, you can use a thumbs-up sign to indicate your support and faith in his capabilities. Generally, children are quite expressive and open in showing their love. They may cuddle up to you, put their arms around your neck or simply climb on to your back as if testing both—the strength of your back and your love. When your child says: 'I love you, Dad,' surely, you feel on top of the world. So, why don't you also express your love and help your child conquer the world.

As a father you can show your love in many ways. If you show respect, affection and concern for your wife, you indirectly convey the same feelings for your children. Apparent affection and harmony between parents is the most reassuring sight for children.

Dare to discipline

There will be occasions when, despite the mother's commanding presence, the father will have to administer the bitter pill of discipline to the child. Almost all parents concede to using some form of physical punishment while disciplining their children. It never creates a rift between them. It is only when children are arbitrarily punished or abused, that problems arise. When disciplining is done fairly and in the context of love, children not only profit but are also less likely to revolt. Whether you stop pocket money, ban television or give a firm slap, disciplining by a loving father is generally effective in correcting a child's behaviour.

There is an old Chinese tale about a father whose son had taken to lying. Each time he was caught in the act, he would promise never to lie again, but with each passing day, he lied more and more until one day his father decided to discipline him. The father caught hold of the son and put him atop a high wooden wardrobe. He asked his son to promise never to lie again or keep sitting on the wardrobe. As was his habit, the son promptly promised not to lie again, without ever meaning it. 'OK!' said father, 'Jump down, I promise I'll catch you.' The son hesitated for a moment but when his father repeated the promise, he jumped down. The father moved back and the son landed on the floor with an almighty crash.

'Do you ever want me to lie to you again?' asked the father. 'No, Father,' replied the son. According to the story, the son never lied again—neither to his father, nor to anyone else.

Make a team with your wife

The successful running of any household depends upon good teamwork between the husband and wife. They need to agree on a set of house rules and then ensure that they are followed. Moreover, a husband must always back up his wife while dealing with indiscipline.

Some fathers try to ingratiate themselves with their children by allowing them to do forbidden things in the absence of their wives. Some even go to the extent of making fun and running down their wives. Fathers who play this game of one-upmanship generally end up as losers. It also holds true for mothers. If a mother thinks her husband is not good enough, her children will also feel the same. On the contrary, a father rated 'Number 1' by the mother—or vice-versa—is usually given the same rating by the children.

No father is perfect. Good fathers are those who work hard to develop the qualities that strengthen family life. They devote equal time to both—building their careers and building their relationship, especially with their children.

36

YOGA FOR CHILDREN

Children these days face a variety of generational challenges which were not present a few decades back. It's not easy to be a kid today. Children have to deal with many distractions, temptations, overstimulation and peer pressure. The emphasis on academic performance and an increasing demand to excel at a host of co-curricular activities at school takes a heavy toll on the child.

Yoga is a low-cost, helpful tool that can have a positive impact on children. A little space and a small mat is all that is required. Compared to other equipment-intensive sports, yoga is ideal for a country like India and is effective, too. Here are some of the main benefits of teaching yoga to children:

Benefits of Yoga

Yoga helps children to:

- Develop body awareness.
- Learn how to exercise their bodies in a healthy way.
- Manage stress by controlling their breathing and through meditation.
- Build concentration, which is very important to perform well in all walks of life.

- Increase their confidence and self-image.
- Feel part of a healthy, non-competitive group.
- Have an alternative to constant attachment to electronic devices. Mobile phones, laptops and gaming devices eat away a major chunk of a child's time, without adding any creative dimension to his personality.

In a school setting, yoga can also benefit teachers by giving them:

- An alternate way to handle challenges in the classroom.
- A healthy activity to integrate with lesson plans.
- A way to make exercising a part of their classes.

Things children can be expected to learn in a yoga class

1. Awareness of the Breath

Breathing exercises can energize kids or encourage relaxation, depending on what type of yoga activity is being taught. Different games and techniques help kids connect to how their bodies feel as a result of deep breathing. Focus increases, as does their breathing and lung capacity. Stress is naturally reduced and healthy hormones (endorphins) are released.

2. Strengthening the Body

It is thought that yoga is great for stretching, but doesn't build strength. It's important for a teacher to emphasize how helpful yoga is for building strength. Talking about the different muscles used in poses, and incorporating games and sequences will help build strength as well as body awareness and coordination. Bodies that are strong, digest and assimilate food better, thereby maintaining a healthy weight. These children grow optimally and can support the stress of carrying heavy loads, like a backpack. They will also breathe better, work more efficiently and protect the more fragile joints.

3. Balancing the Mind

Balancing poses teach children that, with increased focus, they can increase their attention span naturally, even in kids who have problems of short attention span. Poses and games focused on balancing skills develop an intrinsic strength, evoke a meditative feeling, promote stillness and help to quieten the mind. This can help children deal with the stress of living in a chaotic world, where constant stimulation and tension is a regular part of life.

4. Stretching and Lengthening

It's great for kids to be strong, but a body that's only based on strength is not always able to yield under pressure. Strong muscles, without the accompanying flexibility, can't move quickly, pulling on bones and joints. Yoga poses stretch the muscles and by integrating breathing and movement, muscles become warm and more flexible. They can yield when they need to, and support tender joints of children in a more functional way.

5. Awareness and Focus

Yoga helps create an awareness of the body, through deep breathing and movement. It gives children a way to express themselves, and build a strong connection between what they hear and what they do. Children who have a healthy body awareness are more confident and strong, have better posture, breathe better and have a sense of quiet strength. Naturally, they handle stress better and perform well in exams and sports.

6. Flowing, Connecting and Integrating

When we string poses together, we give children a taste of what it means to move with ease. It also helps them build the awareness that all our movements are a series of coordinated efforts between our muscles, bones, joints and nerves. Older children and adolescents are more able to isolate different muscle groups and get more sophisticated about movements. All these things together increase a child's sense of feeling integrated with his body and may help him become an excellent dancer, gymnast, etc.

7. Meditation and Relaxation

Yoga is meditative by nature. So, whether a child is holding a balancing posture, meditating or moving through a series of poses, it is going to provide him a sense of calm. Giving younger kids something to do as they rest on their mats will help with their attention, such as suggesting that they think of a favourite colour or toy. Older children will find it easier to rest longer, with less structure.

There are lots of tools you can use to teach yoga to children. The young ones like games, emulating poses from yoga books for children, and singing songs with big, expressive movements. Older children love to create their own poses, undertake balancing poses which are challenging, and learn about muscles and other aspects of the anatomy.